Get ready for the festive season as Harlequin Romance brings you a Yuletide treat full of Christmas sparkle in this delightful, heartwarming trilogy.

Holiday Miracles

Three sisters discover the magic of Christmas

Join sisters Faith, Hope and Grace Mackinnon as they finally come home to cozy Beckett's Run, a small town with Christmas stockings-full of charm!

Snowbound in the Earl's Castle
Fiona Harper

October 2012

Sleigh Ride with the Rancher
Donna Alward

November 2012

Mistletoe Kisses with the Billionaire
Shirley Jump

December 2012

For Faith, Hope and Grace, this Christmas will be one that they will *never* forget....

Dear Reader,

I've always been fascinated by stained-glass windows. The colors are so bright, almost alive, when a beam of strong sunlight hits the glass. This story centers around one special window in a centuries-old castle. Not only does this colorful glass picture help to unearth a deeply buried family secret, but it brings two very different people together from very different worlds. Their journey to discover the secret behind the window makes them realize that, just like a stained-glass window with no light to make it sing with color, life can be dull and empty without love or faith to make it complete.

The castle in the book is based on the totally amazing Leeds Castle in Kent, which looks as if it's been transported right out of a fairy tale. If you ever get the chance to visit, do. It's only a short train ride from London. If you want to see pictures or find out more about the castle, you can try here: www.leeds-castle.com. Some of the locations in the book are my own invention, but many of the scenes in the book are based on the real castle and its grounds, including the maze and grotto. (Sneaky tip: don't bother with the whole "only make left/right turns" tactic of finding your way to the center. It doesn't work and you'll be going round in circles for hours. Unfortunately, I know this from experience!)

I hope you enjoy reading Faith and Marcus's story. Say a special hello to Basil the Badger for me; he almost became my favorite character!

Blessings,

Fiona Harper

FIONA HARPER

Snowbound in the Earl's Castle

Recycling programs
for this product may
not exist in your area.

ISBN-13: 978-0-373-17837-7

SNOWBOUND IN THE EARL'S CASTLE

First North American Publication 2012

Copyright © 2012 by Fiona Harper

As a child, **Fiona Harper** was constantly teased for either having her nose in a book or living in a dream world. Things haven't changed much since then, but at least in writing she's found a use for her runaway imagination. After studying dance at university, Fiona worked as a dancer, teacher and choreographer, before trading in that career for video editing and production. When she became a mother, she cut back on her working hours to spend time with her children, and when her littlest one started preschool, she found a few spare moments to rediscover an old but not forgotten love—writing.

Fiona lives in London, but her other favorite places to be are the Highlands of Scotland and the Kent countryside on a summer's afternoon. She loves cooking good food and anything cinnamon-flavored. Of course, she still can't keep away from a good book or a good movie—especially romances—but only if she's stocked up with tissues, because she knows she will need them by the end, be it happy or sad. Her favorite things in the world are her wonderful husband, who has learned to decipher her incoherent ramblings, and her two daughters.

Books by Fiona Harper

ALWAYS THE BEST MAN
THE BALLERINA BRIDE
SWEPT OFF HER STILETTOS
THREE WEDDINGS AND A BABY
CHRISTMAS WISHES, MISTLETOE KISSES
BLIND-DATE BABY
INVITATION TO THE BOSS'S BALL
HOUSEKEEPER'S HAPPY-EVER-AFTER
THE BRIDESMAID'S SECRET

Other titles by this author available in ebook format.

For Donna Alward and Shirley Jump.
You girls rock!

And for my editor, Lucy Gilmour, who always
rescues me when I've written myself into a corner.

CHAPTER ONE

THESE were the kind of gates made for keeping people out, Faith thought as she tipped her head back and looked up at twenty feet of twisting and curling black iron. Neither the exquisite craftsmanship nor the sharp wind slicing through the bars did anything to dispel the firm message that outsiders should stay on her side of the gate.

Too bad. She needed to get into the grounds of Hadsborough Castle and she needed to do it today.

She glanced round in frustration to where her Mini sat idling, her suitcase and overnight bag stuffed in the back, and sighed. She'd had other plans for today—ones involving a quaint little holiday cottage on the Kent coast, hot chocolate with marshmallows and a good book. The perfect winter holiday. But that had all changed when she'd found an innocent-looking lilac envelope on her doorstep yesterday morning. The cheerful snowman return address sticker on the back hadn't been fooling anyone. She'd known even before she'd ripped the letter open that its contents would cause trouble, but the exact brand of nuisance had been a total surprise.

She stared out over the top of her Mini to the rolling English countryside beyond. The scene was strangely monochrome. Fog clung to the dips in the fields and everything was tinged with frost. Only the dark silhouettes of trees on top of the hill remained ungilded.

It was strange. She'd grown up in the country back home in Connecticut, but this landscape didn't have the earthy, familiar feel she'd been expecting when she'd driven out of London earlier that morning. Even though she'd adopted this country almost a decade ago, and her sisters now teased her about her so-called British accent, for the first time in ages she was suddenly very aware she was a foreigner. This misty piece of England didn't just feel like another country; it felt like another world.

She turned round and tried a smaller gate beside the main pair, obviously made for foot traffic. No good. Also locked. A painted board at the side of the gate informed her that normal castle opening hours were between ten and four, Tuesday through Saturday. Closed to visitors on Mondays.

But she wasn't a tourist. She had an appointment.

At least she *thought* she had an appointment.

She shook the smaller gate again, and the chain that bound it rattled, laughing back at her.

That was what Gram's letter had said. She pulled the offending article out of her pocket and leafed through the lilac pages, ignoring the smug-looking snowman on the back. She'd bet *he* didn't have a wily old white-haired grandmother who was blackmailing him into taking precious time out of *his* vacation.

She scanned down past the news of Beckett's Run, past Gram's description of how festive her hometown was looking now the residents had started preparing for the annual Christmas Festival.

Ah, here it was.

Faith, honey, I wonder if you'd do me a favor? I have a friend—an old flame, really—who needs help with a stained glass window, and I told him I knew just the girl for the job. Bertie and I were sweethearts after the war. We had a magical summer, but then he went home and

married a nice English girl and I met your grandfather.
I think it all worked out as it should have in the end.

The window is on the estate of Hadsborough Castle
in Kent. What was the name of the man who designed
it? Bertie did say. It'll come to me later...

Anyhow, I know you'll be finished with your London
window soon, and you mentioned the next restoration
project wasn't going to start until the New Year, so I
thought you could go down and help him with it. I told
him you'd be there November 30th at 11 a.m.

And here she was.

Still gripping Gram's letter between thumb and forefinger, she flipped the pages over so she could pull up the sleeve of her grey duffle coat to check her watch. It was the thirtieth, at ten-fifty, so why wasn't anyone here to meet her? To let her in? She could have been sipping hot chocolate right now if it hadn't been for Gram's little idea of a detour.

As beautiful as the window at St Bede's in Camden had looked when the team had finished restoring it, it had been four months of back-breaking, meticulous labour. She deserved a break, and she was going to have it.

Just as soon as she'd checked out this window.

She turned the last page over and looked below her grandmother's signature. Reading the line again still gave her goosebumps.

P.S. I knew it would come to me! Samuel Crowbridge.
That was the designer's name.

Without that tantalising mention of the well-known British artist Faith would have blown off this little side trip on the way to her holiday cottage in a heartbeat.

Well...okay, maybe she'd have come anyway. Gram had been the one stable figure in her otherwise chaotic childhood—more like a surrogate mother than a grandparent. All Faith's happiest memories were rooted in Gram's pretty little house in Beckett's Run. She owed her grandmother big time, and she'd probably have danced on one leg naked in the middle of Trafalgar Square if the old lady had asked her to.

She supposed she should be grateful that the letter hadn't started, *Faith, honey, try not to get arrested, but could you just hop down to Nelson's Column and...?*

The road that passed the castle entrance was quiet, but at that moment she heard the noise of a car engine and turned round. Thankfully, a Land Rover had pulled in beside her and the driver rolled down the passenger window.

'It's closed today,' the man in a chunky-knit sweater said, in a not-unfriendly manner.

Faith nodded. 'I have an appointment to see…' This was the moment she realised Gram had neglected to reveal her old flame's full name. 'Bertie?'

The man in the car frowned slightly. He didn't look convinced.

'It's about the window,' she added, not really expecting it to help. The appointment her grandmother had made for her seemed as flimsy and insubstantial as the disappearing mist. But the man nodded.

'Follow me in,' he said. 'There's a public car park just up the road. You can walk the rest of the way from there.'

'Thanks,' she replied, and got back into her car.

Five minutes later, after a drive through the most stunning parkland, she was standing beside her Mini as the noise of the Land Rover's engine faded. She watched the four-wheel drive disappear round a corner, then followed the path the man had indicated in the opposite direction, up a gentle slope of close-cropped grass. When she got to the top of the hill she stopped dead in her tracks and her mouth fell open.

Beyond an expansive lawn, gauzy mist hung above a dark, mirror-like lake. Above it, almost as if it was floating above the surface of the water, was the most stunning castle she'd ever seen. It was made of large blocks of creamy sandstone, crested with crenellations, and finished off with a turret or two for good measure. Long, narrow windows punctuated its walls.

The castle enclosure stretched from the bank on her right across two small islands. A plain single-track bridge joined the first island to the shore, guarded by a gatehouse. The smaller island was a fortified keep, older than the rest of the castle, and joined to the newer, larger wing by a two-storey arched bridge.

The whole thing looked like something out of a fairytale. Better than anything she'd dreamed up when Gram had tucked her and her sisters in at night on their summer holidays and read to them out of Faith's favourite fabric-covered storybook.

She started to walk, hardly caring that she'd left the Tarmac, and started off across the dew-laden grass, running the risk of getting goose poop on her boots. The edge of the lake was fringed with reeds, and a pair of black swans with scarlet beaks drifted around each other, totally oblivious to her presence.

That bridge from the bank to the gatehouse seemed to be the only way to get to the rest of the castle, so she guessed she might as well start there. Perhaps there would be someone on duty who knew where this window or the mysterious Bertie could be found.

She was nearing the castle, walking close to the low-lying bank, when she saw a dark shape in the mist moving towards her. She stopped and pulled her coat tighter around her. The damp air clung to her cheeks.

She could make out a figure—long, tall and dark. A man, his coat flapping behind him as he strode towards her. She was inevitably reminded of stern Victorian gentlemen in gothic novels. There was something about the purpose in his stride, the way his collar was turned up. But then he came closer and she could see clearly from his thick ribbed sweater and the dark jeans under his overcoat that he was a product of this century after all.

He hadn't noticed her. She knew she ought to say something, call out, but she couldn't seem to breathe, let alone talk.

She had the oddest feeling that she recognised him, although she couldn't have explained just which of his features were familiar. It was all of them. All of *him*. And him being in this place.

Which was crazy, because she'd never been here before in her life—except maybe in her childish daydreams—and she'd certainly remember meeting a man like this…a man whose sudden appearance answered a question she wasn't aware she'd asked.

Finally he spotted her, and his stride faltered for a moment, but then his spine lengthened and he carried on, his focus narrowing to her and only her. The look in his eyes reminded her of a hunting dog that had just picked up a scent.

'Hey!' he called out as came closer.

'Hi…' Faith tried to say, but the damp air muffled the word, and the noise that emerged from her mouth was hardly intelligible.

He was only a few feet away now, and Faith stuffed her gloved hands into her coat pockets as she tipped her head back to look him in the face. My, he was tall. But not burly with it. Long and lean. She could see why she'd had that dumb notion about him now. Black hair, slightly too long to be tidy, flopped over his forehead and curled at his collar. His bone structure and long, straight nose spoke of centuries of breeding and he addressed her now in a manner that left her in no doubt that he was used to having people do as he said.

'The castle and grounds are closed to visitors today. You'll have to turn round and go back the way you came.'

And he stood there, waiting for her to obey him.

Normally Faith didn't have any problem being polite and accommodating, doing what she was asked—it was the path to a quiet and peaceful existence after all—but there was something about his tone, about the way he hadn't even stopped to ask if she had a valid reason for being there, that just riled her up. Maybe it was the suggestion that once again she was somewhere she didn't belong that made her temper rise.

'I'm not trespassing. I'm supposed to—'

Before she could finish her sentence he took another step forward, cupped his hand under her elbow and started to walk her back in the direction she'd just come.

'Hey!' she said, and yanked her elbow out of his grip. 'Hands off, buddy!'

'Should have known it,' he muttered, almost to himself. 'American tourists are always the worst.' Then he spoke louder, and more slowly, as if he were talking to a child. 'Listen, you have to realise this isn't just a visitor attraction like Disneyland. It's a family home, too, and we have just as much right to our privacy as anyone else. Now, if you don't leave quietly I will be forced to call the police.'

Faith was rapidly losing the urge even to be polite to this stuck-up…whoever he was. No matter how dashing he'd looked walking out of the mist.

'No, *you* listen,' she replied firmly. 'I have every right to be here. I have an appointment with Bertie.'

He stopped herding her towards the exit and his eyes narrowed further. She had no doubt that a sharp mind went hand in hand with those aristocratic looks. 'You mean Albert Huntington?'

Faith took a split second longer than she would have liked to reply. 'Yes, of course.' There couldn't be more than one Albert—Bertie—around this place, could there? That had to be him.

Unfortunately Mr Tall, Dark and Full of Himself didn't

miss a trick. He spotted her hesitation and instantly grabbed her arm again, started marching her back towards the gate. 'Nice try, but nobody but the family calls him Bertie—and you're from the wrong continent entirely to be considered a close relation.'

Hah. That was all he knew.

'Actually, my father is as English as you are,' she added icily. 'And my grandmother—' the American one, but she didn't mention that '—is an old friend of his. I'm here to give my professional opinion on a stained glass window!'

He let go of her arm and turned to look her up and down. '*You're* the expert Bertie's asked to look at the window?'

Close enough to the truth. She nodded. 'I believe it might need some kind of repair.'

Okay, she didn't actually know if any restoration work was needed, but why would Gram have sent her here otherwise? It was a pretty good guess, and she really, *really* wanted to sneak a look at that window at least once before this man frogmarched her off the estate. Not one of Crowbridge's other windows—and there hadn't been many—had survived the Blitz. This could be a significant discovery.

He stopped looking irritated and purposeful, closed his eyes and ran a hand through his dark hair before glancing back in the direction of the castle. 'I hoped he'd given up on that idea.' He gave her a weary look. 'I suppose I'd better take you to meet him, then, Miss…?'

'McKinnon. Faith McKinnon,' she said, trying to get her voice to remain even.

'I apologise, Miss McKinnon, if I've been a little abrupt…'

A *little?* And he didn't look that sorry to her. If anything he'd clenched up further. Her younger sister would have described him as having a stick up his—

'I'm sure you can understand how difficult it is to have your home invaded,' he added, but Faith still wasn't quite sure she was off the 'invader' list.

'People think that because we open our home to them for a few days each week it is somehow public property.'

She nodded. She knew all about invading families, about being a cuckoo in the nest, but she wasn't going to tell *this* man that. It certainly wouldn't endear her to him any further.

'Bertie isn't in the best of health at the moment,' he added gravely. 'I've been trying to make sure he doesn't get too upset.' He led the way back through the thinning mist round the edge of the lake. 'Difficult, though,' he added, 'when he's obsessed with this damn window.'

He strode ahead, and Faith followed him up a short incline and onto the first, plainer stone bridge, through a large arch under the gatehouse and onto an oval lawn that filled more than half of the first castle island. She tried not to let her eyes pop out of her head.

Wow.

The castle was even better close up than it had been rising through the mist. A gravel pathway encircled the lawn and led up to a vast front door covered in iron studs.

This Bertie had his office in the castle itself? *Nice.*

As her guide opened the front door and stood aside to let her pass, he surprised her by allowing one side of his mouth to hitch up in the start of a smile as he checked his watch.

'I imagine Bertie will be finished with his morning tea by now. I'll take you through to the drawing room.'

Faith looked at him sharply. 'You mean Bertie *lives* here?'

The almost-smile disappeared. 'Of course he lives here. It's his home.' He shook his head. 'You Americans really do have some funny ideas, you know...'

Faith held her breath. She would have liked to challenge him on that last comment, but two things stopped her. First, it would have given her lack of knowledge about this Bertie away. Second, she was too busy making sense of all the mismatched pieces of information running round her head.

Gram had left a heck of a lot out of her letter, hadn't she?

She cleared her throat. 'Does Bertie have a full title?'

He gave her the patronising kind of look that told her he thought she'd finally started asking sensible questions. 'Albert Charles Baxter Huntington, seventh Duke of Hadsborough.'

Faith blinked slowly, trying to give nothing away.

Act like you knew that.

A duke? Gram had had a fling with a *duke?* She'd thought from the tone of the letter that he'd been a fellow academic or master craftsman working on a project. She hadn't even considered that Bertie might *own* the window. And the building it inhabited. And this castle. And probably most of the land for miles around. Part of her was shocked at her conservative grandmother's secret past. Another part wanted to punch the air and say, *Go, Gram!*

Faith's throat was suddenly very dry. 'And that would make you…?'

He frowned, then held out his hand, doing nothing to erase the horizontal lines that were bunching up his forehead. 'Marcus Huntington—estate manager of Hadsborough Castle…'

Faith looked at his hand and swallowed. Hesitantly, she pulled her hand from her mitten and slid it into his. Since he hadn't been wearing gloves she'd expected his skin to be ice-cold, but his grip was firm and his palm was warm against hers.

She looked down at their joined hands. This felt right. As if she remembered doing this before and had been waiting to do it again. Worse than that, she didn't want to let go. She looked back up at him, hoping she didn't look as panic-stricken as she felt. That was when her heart really started to thump.

He was staring at their hands, too. Then he looked up and his eyes met hers. She saw matching confusion and surprise in his expression.

He cleared his throat. 'Bertie's grandson and heir.'

* * *

Marcus pulled his hand away from hers, ignoring the pleasant ripple of sensation as her fingertips brushed his palm. Not the cliché of an electric shock racing up his arm. No, something far more unsettling—a sense of warmth, a sense of how right her hand felt in his. And that couldn't be, because everything about this situation was wrong. She was not supposed to be here, trespassing on his family's lives and stirring up trouble.

But it hadn't been just the touch. It had started before that, when he'd caught her walking down by the lake. There was something about those small, understated features and those direct, *reasonable* brown eyes that totally caught him off guard.

And if there was one thing he hated it was being off guard.

However, when she'd slid her hand into his, and all the ear-pounding had stopped and his senses had calmed down and come to rest…

If anything that had been worse.

He couldn't let himself fall into that trap again, so it was time to do something about it. Time to find out what Faith McKinnon wanted and deal with her as quickly as possible.

'If you'll follow me…?'

He turned and led the way through a flagstone-paved entrance hall, its arches and whitewashed walls decorated with remnants of long-ago disassembled suits of armour, then showed her into the yellow drawing room—the smallest and warmest reception room on the ground floor of the castle.

Gold-coloured damask covered the walls, fringed with heavy brocade tassels under the plaster coving at the top. There were antique tables covered in trinkets and family photographs, a grand piano, and a large squashy sofa in front of the vast marble fireplace. Off to one side of the hearth, in a high-backed leather armchair, reading his daily newspaper, was his grandfather. He looked so innocent. No one would guess he'd ignited a bit of a family row with this window obsession.

Marcus wasn't exactly sure what the kerfuffle was about—something that had happened decades earlier, in a time when stiff-lipped silence had been the preferred solution to every problem—but his great-aunt Tabitha had warned him that Bertie was about to open a Pandora's box of trouble, and nothing any of them learned about whatever the family had been keeping quiet for more than half a century would make anyone any happier.

Disruption was the last thing he needed—especially as he'd spent the last couple of years getting everything back on an even keel. Bertie might live at Hadsborough now, but in his younger years he'd all but abandoned his duty to explore the world.

Unfortunately he'd passed his *laissez-faire* attitude down to his only son, and before his death Marcus's father had just seen the castle as somewhere impressive to bring his business friends for the odd weekend. He'd also failed to keep hold of three wives, and the resulting divorce settlements had crippled the family finances further. But that was just the tip of the iceberg where his father had been concerned. It had taken centuries to build this family's reputation, and his father had managed to rip it to shreds within twelve months.

So Marcus had left the City and come to Hadsborough to be by his grieving grandfather's side. It was his job to claw it all back now. The Huntington family legacy had been neglected for too many generations. Taken for granted. These things couldn't just be left to run their own course; they needed to be managed. Guarded. Or there would be nothing left—not even a good name—to pass on to his children when they came along.

'Grandfather?'

The old man looked up from his paper, the habitual twinkle in his eye. Marcus nodded towards their guest.

'I found Miss McKinnon, here, wandering in the grounds. I believe *you* are expecting her?'

If his grandfather had heard the extra emphasis in his grandson's words he gave no sign he'd registered it. He carefully folded his paper, placed it on the table next to him, rose unsteadily to his feet and offered his hand to the stranger in their drawing room.

'Miss McKinnon,' he said, smiling. 'Delighted to meet you.'

The old charmer, Marcus thought.

Faith McKinnon smiled politely and shook his hand. 'Hi,' she said. If she was charmed she didn't show it.

'Thank you for coming at such short notice,' his grandfather said as he lowered himself carefully back into his chair. 'If you don't mind me saying, you resemble your grandmother.'

The blank, businesslike expression on Faith McKinnon's face was replaced with one of surprise. 'Really? Th-thank you.'

Marcus frowned. She'd been telling the truth, then. Yet the reliable hairs at the back of his neck had informed him she'd been lying about something.

Why was she puzzled that someone had said she resembled a family member? He glanced at the portrait of the third Duke over the mantelpiece and raised his fingers absentmindedly to touch the bridge of his nose. There was no escaping that distinctive feature in the Huntington family line. They all had it. Genetics had branded them and marked them as individual connections in a long chain. And, as the only direct heir, Marcus was determined not to be the weak link that ended the line.

He turned to his grandfather. 'Miss McKinnon tells me you knew her grandmother?'

Before his grandfather could answer their guest interrupted. 'Call me Faith, please.'

Bertie nodded and smiled back at her. 'Mary and I were

sweethearts for a time when I was in America after the war,'
his grandfather said. 'She was an exceptional woman.'

Marcus turned sharply to look at him. Sweethearts? He'd
never heard this before—never heard mention of a romance
before his grandmother. It made him realise just *how* silent
his family stayed on certain matters, that maybe he didn't
know everything about his own history.

'Please do sit down, Miss McK…Faith,' his grandfather
said.

She chose the edge of the sofa, her knees pressed together
and her hands in her lap. Marcus would have been quite content to remain standing, but he felt as if he was towering
above the other two, somehow excluded from what they were
about to discuss, so he dropped into the armchair opposite
his grandfather, crossing one long leg over the other. But he
couldn't get comfortable, as he would have done if it had just
been him and his grandfather alone as usual.

'So, Grandfather…what has all this got to do with the window?'

At the mention of the window Miss McKinnon's eyes widened and she leaned forward. 'Gram said you need help with
it?'

Marcus kept on watching her. Her voice was low and calm,
but behind her speech was something else. As if his words
had lit a fire inside her. *Interesting.* Just exactly what was
she hoping to gain from this situation? He wouldn't have
pegged her for a con artist or a gold-digger, but they came
in all shapes and sizes. Stepmothers one and two had proved
that admirably.

His grandfather nodded. 'It's in a chapel on the estate
here. I wouldn't have thought any more of it, except that a
few months ago my father's younger brother died, and his
widow found some letters my father had written to him in
his personal effects. She wondered if I'd like to see them.'

Marcus squinted slightly. Yes, that would make sense. Now

he thought about it, he realised it *had* been around that time that Grandfather had started muttering to himself and begun hiding himself away in the library, poring over old papers.

Bertie stared into the crackling fire in the grate. 'My father died when I was very young, you see, and she thought I might get more of a sense of who he was through them.'

Marcus resisted the urge to scowl. After his recent heart surgery, and with his soaring blood pressure, the doctors had said his grandfather needed rest and quiet. No stress. They had definitely not prescribed getting all stirred up about a family mystery—if indeed there was one. It would be best to leave it all alone, let time settle like silt over those memories until they were buried. There had been enough scandal in the present. They didn't need extra dredged up from the past.

Pursuing this thing with the window was a bad idea on so many levels. That was why he intended to get the facts out of his grandfather quickly and show this Miss McKinnon the blasted window, if that was what she really wanted. Because the sooner she was off the estate and he could get things back to normal the better.

CHAPTER TWO

FAITH frowned. While Bertie—she couldn't quite get used to thinking of this gentle old man as a duke—was charming, she didn't see what his family history had to do with anything.

'I'm sorry…but how does this connect to the window in the chapel?'

At least she knew that much now. A church window. Next task was to gauge how old it was.

Bertie was staring into the fire again. She had the feeling he'd wandered off into his own memories. Perhaps that was nice, if you had a solid and well-adjusted family as he had, but in Faith's view the less time she spent thinking about her family the better. They certainly didn't make her feel all warm and fuzzy and wistful.

When all three McKinnon sisters got together none of them behaved like the mature women they were; they regressed to childhood, resurrecting deeply embedded hurts and resentments, filtering every word through their past history. It was always the same, no matter how hard Gram pleaded, or how hard they tried to make it different each time. And when they added their flaky mother into the mix—well…

Bertie seemed to shake himself out of his reverie. 'The original window was damaged during a storm almost a hundred years ago, and my father commissioned a new one to be made.'

'And it needs restoration?'

The old man shrugged. 'There does seem to be a little irregularity down at the bottom.'

So maybe it was all about establishing the history of the window—just what she was interested in herself. 'My grandmother says you know who did the design?'

Another shrug. 'Samuel Someone-or-other. I forget the last name.' He stopped looking at her and his gaze wandered back to the fire.

'Crowbridge,' she said. 'Samuel Crowbridge.'

And if Gram was right—if Crowbridge really *had* designed Bertie's window—it would be the stained glass version of finding King Tut's tomb. He'd only ventured into making windows late in his life, and none of the few examples remained. At least that was what everybody had thought...

She caught Marcus's eye. His expression was unreadable, but he seemed to be watching her very carefully, as if he was expecting her to make a sudden move. Unfortunately, as well as the spike of irritation that shot through her at his superior, *entitled* study of her, there was a fizz of something much more pleasurable in her veins. She looked away.

She turned her attention back to his grandfather. 'Mr... I mean, Your—' She stopped, embarrassed at her lack of knowledge about what to call her host. *Your Dukeness* just didn't sound right in her head.

'Bertie is fine,' the older man said. 'I never did like all that nonsense.'

Marcus shook his head slightly at his grandfather's response. Faith knew what she wanted to call *him,* whether he had a proper title or not. She sat up straighter. The grandson might have the looks—and some weird *déjà vu* thing going on—but she'd prefer Bertie's company any day. She could totally understand why Gram had been so taken with him once.

'Well, *Bertie*—' she shot a look at his grandson '—if you don't want the window repaired or evaluated, I'm not sure why I'm here.' She hoped desperately he'd let her see it any-way—if only for a few moments.

Bertie's eyes began to shine and he leaned forward. 'You, my dear, are going to help me unravel a mystery.'

'A mystery?' she repeated slowly. She tried to sound neu-tral, but it came out sounding suspicious and cynical.

He nodded. 'My mother left Hadsborough three years after my father died. I was always told that he'd married beneath himself, in both station and character, and that she hadn't wanted to be stuck out in the countryside in a draughty heap of stones with a screaming child.'

Faith felt a familiar tug of sympathy inside her ribcage, but she ignored it, sat up straighter and blinked. She wasn't going to get sucked in. She wasn't going to get involved. She was here for the window and that was all.

'I'm sure you were a cute baby,' was all she said.

Bertie chuckled. 'By all accounts I was a terror. Anyway, I was also told my father realised his mistake soon after the wedding. But people didn't get divorced in those days, you see…'

Faith nodded—even though she didn't really see. Her own mother had never felt tied by any strings of convention. If it had felt good she'd done it—and it had ripped her family apart. Maybe there was something to be said for doing your duty, sitting back and putting up with stuff, just so every-one else didn't have to ride the tidal wave of consequences with you.

'I have a feeling my uncle Reginald didn't approve of my father's choice of bride, so my father doesn't mention her much in these letters, but I get the impression my parents were happy together.'

Faith could feel her curiosity rising. *Don't bite the bait,* she told herself. *Family squabbles are trouble. Best avoided. Best run away from.*

'And does he mention the window in the letters?'

Bertie grinned. 'Oh, yes.' He pulled some yellowing sheets of paper from a leather folder that he'd tucked down the side of his chair and leafed through them. 'He wrote of his plans to rebuild the window to his brother. He seemed very excited about it.' The smile disappeared from his face as he stopped and stared at one short letter. 'He even mentioned it in his final letter.' He looked up. 'He survived the Great War, but died of flu the following year. This letter is the last one he wrote from hospital.'

He reached forward and offered the letter to Faith. Knowing it would probably pain him to get up, she rose and took it from him. She walked towards the fire and tried to make sense of the untidy scrawl. This was obviously the last communication of a man gripped by fever. The content was mostly family-related, which Faith skipped through. It wasn't her business, even if she *was* starting to feel a certain sympathy for Bertie and his tragic father. She knew all about tragic fathers, be they dead or merely missing from one's life.

'Read the last paragraph,' Bertie prompted.

Faith turned the page over and found it.

It was supposed to be a grand surprise, Reggie, but I don't suppose I'll get the chance to do it properly now. Tell Evie there's a message for her. Tell her to look in the window.

Marcus stood up and strode across to where Faith was standing. He held out a hand, almost demanding the letter. She raised an eyebrow and made a point of reading it through one more time before handing it over.

He shook his head as he read. 'Grandfather, you can't put any stock in this. These are clearly the wanderings of a delirious mind.'

Bertie shook his head. 'It's all starting to come together… bits and pieces of conversations I've heard over the years…

strange comments the servants made… I think my father loved my mother a lot more than I've been led to believe, and I want to know why she left—why the family would never talk about her.'

Faith withdrew from the warmth of the fire and sat back down on the edge of the sofa. She was more confused than ever. 'I can understand that, Bertie…'

If anyone could understand it would be her—to have the security of knowing one parent hadn't deserted you and the other hadn't deceived you—she would have given anything to return to that wonderful state of bliss before she'd uncovered her own family's secret.

'But what does it have to do with me?'

He looked at her intently, his face serious. 'You know about stained glass, about its traditions and imagery. I've stared at that damn window for hours in the last couple of weeks and I'll be blasted if I can see anything there.'

He leaned forward and lowered his voice, and Faith couldn't help tilting forward to mirror him.

'I want you to find the clue my father left for my mother, Faith. I want you to find the message in the window.'

Her heart was hammering. She told herself it was from keeping up with Marcus Huntington's blistering pace as he escorted her to the chapel. An outsider like her couldn't be trusted to look at it on her own, of course.

She glanced at the sky above and realised she recognised that particular shade of grey. Snow was on its way. But a bit of snow didn't worry her. Or even a whole bunch of it. Beckett's Run had plenty every year. But Beckett's Run knew how to deal with it. A few flakes and this country ground to a halt. So she wanted to be tucked up in her little holiday cottage with a stiff salty breeze blowing off the North Sea if it really decided to come down. Which meant she needed to get to work fast—something the man striding ahead of her would no doubt appreciate.

The path they'd been following led them through some trees and into a pretty hollow with a clearing. In the centre was a smaller version of a traditional English stone church. The grass under their feet must once have been a lawn, but it now rose knee-high, and the ground was lumpy with thick clumps of rye grass. Shrubs grew wild, bowed down with the weight of their unpruned branches. Some clung to the walls of the chapel to support themselves. Compared to the rest of the estate, this little corner appeared unkempt and uncared for.

Faith wasn't one for believing in fairy stories. Not any more. And she had the feeling that Bertie, lovely as he was, had the capacity to spin a tall tale or two, but there was something about this little hidden part of the estate that made her wonder if the Huntingtons had deliberately neglected it.

She watched Marcus stride up to the heavy oak door ahead of her and shivered. Twenty-eight years old, and she'd never had a reaction to a man like this before. It was downright freaky.

Pure attraction she could have handled, but this was different. There was more to it. Extra layers below the fizzle of awareness. Pity she was too much of a coward to peel back the top layer and see what lay underneath.

Marcus slid a key into the black iron lock and turned it. He pushed the door open and motioned for her to go inside, stepping back out of the way so there was no danger of them passing within even three feet of each other.

It wouldn't do her much good to peel back that layer, anyway. He didn't want her here. The vibe emanated from him in waves, like a silent broadcast,

She turned back to watch him as he pulled the door closed and followed her inside. He caught her eye and immediately looked away.

She wasn't the only coward.

He felt it, too. She knew he did. But he wanted it even less than her physical presence on his territory, and Faith wasn't going to push it. No point trying to wriggle yourself into somewhere you didn't belong.

She followed him inside, blinking a few times to adjust her eyes to the relative gloom. As always when she entered a church her eyes were drawn immediately to the windows at either end. Hardly able to help it, she ignored where her host was trying to lead her and veered off to stare at the multi-paned window at the back of the church near the door.

Soft light filtered through the glass, filling the dusty interior with colour. She held her breath. Both the glass picture high on the wall and the afternoon sun were beautiful in their own right, but when they met…it was magic.

Their entrance had disturbed a hundred million dust motes, and now the specks danced in the light, as if an unseen artist had painstakingly coloured each one a different shade. And not only did the shapes and pictures in the window sing, but some of that colour—that life—pierced the darkness of the sanctuary on beams of light, leaving kaleidoscope shadows where it fell.

She sighed, even though she could tell at a glance that this was not the window Bertie had been talking about. Too old. A nineteenth-century creation featuring Bible characters dressed in medieval garb. Didn't matter. She was still captivated. These grand scenes always reminded her of the coloured plates from her favourite storybook as a child—noble men and beautiful ladies in flowing, heavy robes, bright lush pastures and an achingly blue heaven above.

'It's over here,' a voice said from somewhere close to the altar.

Faith took one last look at the window and turned, screwing her 'don't care' face back in place as she did so, and walked towards where Marcus Huntington was standing, hands in his pockets.

As she walked down the aisle she looked around. It was obvious someone had been trying to tidy the place up, but there was still a long way to go. Nothing a mop and a bucket and some elbow grease wouldn't sort out, though.

'We plan to reopen the chapel this year and have a Carol Service here,' he explained, then stooped into a smaller niche in a side wall, revealing a much smaller stained glass window. He stepped back to give her access, but turned his intense stare her direction. 'So...what do you think?'

Faith took a few paces towards the narrow window. It was maybe a foot wide and six feet high, with typical Gothic revival tracery at the top. Her heart began to pump. Could this really be it?

The glass was all rich colours and delicate paintwork: a fair-haired woman knelt praying at the bottom of the picture, her palms pressed together, face upturned, eyes fixed on the blaze of celestial glory at the top of the window. She was surrounded by flowers and shrubs, and a small dog sat at her feet, gazing at her in much the same way she was gazing at the heavens. It was stunning. And unusual. More like a painting in its composition than a church window.

There was something in the woman's face... Something about her expression of pure joy that made Faith want to lean in and touch her—see if she could absorb some of that emotion by pure osmosis. Truly, the window was enchanting.

She turned round to see what her reluctant host could tell her about it and bumped into something warm and solid. She'd been aware that he'd been standing behind her, but not that he'd stepped in closer.

'S-sorry!' she stuttered, finding herself staring into his chest.

'Well?' he asked, a hint of impatience in his tone.

She knew she really ought to step back, move away, but her gaze had snagged on a feathery piece of cobweb that was stuck in his hair just above his right temple. For some reason she was suddenly much more interested in reaching up and gently brushing it away than turning round and looking at the coloured glass and lead she'd been so desperate to set eyes on.

What was even more worrying was the fact that she'd almost done it anyway—as if she'd known him long enough to share that easy kind of intimacy. It seemed unnatural *not* to.

Breathe, Faith. Turn around. Just because he looks like a modern-day Prince Charming it doesn't mean you should audition for the role of Cinderella. That would be a really dumb idea.

He frowned, followed her gaze, and discovered the cobweb on his own. He brushed it away with long fingers and then did the oddest thing: he chuckled softly. To himself, though. None of the humour was to be shared with her. But it changed his face completely, softening the angular planes, and made him seem younger, less stand-offish. Faith discovered she'd stopped breathing.

No. Don't you do it, Faith McKinnon. Don't you believe where there's no hope. You learned those lessons young. You're not that soft-hearted girl any more, remember?

She didn't smile back at him, but turned abruptly and stared at the window again. He moved away, thank goodness, walked closer to the window to inspect it for himself. They remained silent for a few minutes, both focused intently on the gently lit glass picture in front of them.

Marcus came and stood beside her. 'For a long time all the windows here were boarded up. I don't think I've ever taken a really good look at this before. It's actually quite beautiful.'

Faith nodded, still staring at the golden-haired woman. 'If I lived here I'd come to see it every day.'

He folded his arms and looked around. 'This chapel hasn't been used by the family for decades. No one has been here much since—' He stopped short, as if a jagged thunderbolt of a thought had just hit him, and then turned to look at her. 'Since my grandfather was a small boy.'

She met his gaze. 'You think there's a link? Something to do with what your grandfather said earlier?'

He pressed his lips together. 'There could be any one of a dozen reasons why the family has left this place alone. For a start, I don't think any of my immediate ancestors were very religious.'

He wasn't going to budge an inch, was he? On anything. He was right and everyone else was wrong. That chapped her hide. He reminded her so much of her older sister, always issuing orders as if they were divine decrees.

She folded her arms across her chest. 'You don't believe him, do you?'

He was silent for a few seconds, and then turned his attention back to the stained glass window. 'I believe there was some big family ruckus—probably a storm in a teacup—but as for there being a secret message in the window... It seems a little far-fetched.' He sighed. 'I think it's what my grandfather *wants* to believe.'

Faith chewed the side of her lip. No pressure, then. It was just up to her to confirm or crush an old man's dreams. She stepped forward again and focused once more on the subject of all the controversy.

'See anything out of the ordinary?' he asked.

She tipped her head to the side. 'It's difficult to say. Despite the subject matter, it isn't a very typical design for a church.'

She pulled a sheaf of photographs out of her bag and held them up so she could compare them against the window. They were images of various paintings and sketches of the supposed artist's other lost windows. 'It's similar to Crowbridge's earlier work, which was heavily influenced by the Pre-Raphaelite Brotherhood.'

He nodded. 'This window certainly has a touch of that style.'

Faith's brows rose a notch and she swivelled her eyes to look at him. 'You know something about art?' What a relief to find he knew about something other than ordering people around, making them feel unwanted.

He gave her a derisive look.

She ignored it and cleared her throat. 'But his work changed dramatically after the turn of the last century. This window isn't anything like the paintings he was producing around the time this window was made.'

A lead weight settled inside her stomach. She hadn't realised it, but she'd been dumb enough to let herself get excited about the window, to let herself hope. She turned away from it, wanting to block the image out for a second.

She should have been smarter than to get sucked in to the fantasy like that. But it was this place... Hadsborough was a like a fairytale on steroids. It was hard *not* to fall into that trap. She would just have to do better in the future.

'I can see how an amateur might have made the error,' she said, looking Marcus in the eye, 'but I don't think Samuel Crowbridge made this window.'

'You know your subject, Miss McKinnon.'

'Nice of you to notice,' she replied. Really, the nerve of the man. She didn't need his validation. 'And it's *Faith*.'

He blinked slowly, as if he'd registered her request and would think it over. Faith didn't usually have a short fuse, but something about this man, his superior attitude, just drove her nuts.

'Any sign of this message my grandfather mentioned?'

She shook her head, although she wanted to say, *Yes, it's there in letters three feet high,* just to get up his nose. 'Nothing pops out, but since it's not a traditional church window the normal symbolic conventions may not apply.'

'I need to know for sure,' Marcus said. 'My grandfather will just keep fretting about it unless you give me something more concrete.'

She thought of the charming old man, sitting by the fire, trying to read his newspaper while he waited for her to give him hope where there was none. But Bertie had asked for her professional opinion, hadn't he? And she needed to honour that—stay dispassionate, objective. It wasn't her fault if it had all been a dead end.

Don't get involved...

Right. That was what she was going to do. Not get involved.

It wasn't normally a problem in her line of work. The people intimately connected with the windows she worked on were long dead, shrouded in the mystery of another century. So this window was a little different, had a sad story to go along with it. That shouldn't change anything. It didn't.

'I could do some further research,' she said. 'I should be able to send you a report in a couple of days, but I don't think it's going to turn up anything new.'

He breathed out, looking slightly thankful. 'Maybe that's for the best.' He glanced over his shoulder to the open door. 'Thank you, Miss McKinnon.'

Still with the 'Miss McKinnon'. He used her name like a shield.

She took one last look at the window. It really was beautiful—so unusual. And apart from the bad repair job down at the bottom it was in good condition. It was sad to leave it that way, especially when it wouldn't be a long job—not like the one she'd just finished...

Marcus moved towards the door. 'We'd better go back and talk to the Duke,' he said, not bothering to look over his shoulder.

Right. And then it would be time to get back to where she belonged—her own world, her own life.

CHAPTER THREE

Marcus stayed silent when they reached the drawing room, while Bertie insisted Faith have another cup of tea before she continued on her journey. She perched on the edge of the sofa again, and began to explain carefully what she'd found.

He noticed that she worked up to breaking the bad news, and he was grateful to her for that. He was pleased she hadn't just blurted it all out as soon as she'd walked into the room. As far as he'd seen Faith McKinnon had a gift for bluntness. It was reassuring to know that a little sensitivity lay underneath.

He brushed beads of moisture from his shoulders as he stood by the fireplace. Fine flakes of snow, almost dust-like, had fallen on them on their walk back from the chapel and now melted from the warmth of the flames. He looked out of the window over the lake. Snow. That was the last thing they needed right now. Hadsborough lay in a dip in the land, and it was always much worse here than in the nearby towns and villages. Still, it was ten years since they'd had anything but a few inches. He was probably worrying for nothing.

He found himself doing that a lot these days. Churning things over in his mind. Wondering in the middle of the night if there was anything he had missed. It was as if he tried to outrun his own personal cloud of doom all day by keeping busy, and then it would settle over him while he slept, poisoning his dreams.

Some nights, in a half dream-state, he'd travel further into the past, endlessly trying to relive moments that would never come again. He'd try to make the right decision this time, hoping he'd prevent the coming tragedy, that he could save his father from both disgrace and the grave, but when the sun rose in the morning all his nocturnal fretting hadn't changed anything.

He should have done more. Foolishly trusting his father, he'd seen it all happening and yet stood by, believing his father's assurances when he should have doubted them. But he wasn't going to make that mistake again; he had his eyes open now.

And not just when it came to family; when it came to *everything*. He should have realised that the woman he'd trusted with everything he'd had left—which hadn't been much— would eventually sit him down and tell him it was all too much for her, that she would leave him on his own to bear all the new responsibility that had come his way while she skipped off to a life of freedom. He'd given himself completely to a woman who hadn't known the meaning of loyalty, who hadn't known how to stand by the people she loved. How had he been so blind?

At least his relationship with Amanda had taught him something important, something the storybooks and the love songs failed to mention—love was always an unequal proposition. One person always gave more, always cared more, was always ready to sacrifice more. And that person was the weaker, more vulnerable side of the equation. One thing he was certain of: he was never going to be that person again.

'I'm sorry I didn't find what you were looking for,' he heard Faith say, and he realised he'd missed some of the conversation.

He lifted his head to look at her. Her face and eyes were totally expressionless. Too expressionless. A casual observer might have thought she didn't care, that she was handing out platitudes, but he recognised that look on her face. It was the one he saw every morning in the mirror when he made sure his own walls were still securely in place. They were more alike than he'd thought.

His grandfather nodded, trying not to look despondent. There was a flinch, a moment of hesitation, and then Faith reached over and covered his hand with hers. And then she smiled. It was the first hint of a smile he'd seen from her all day, and rather than being brassy and bright and false this one was soft and shy. Something inside his chest kicked.

But then the smile was gone, and Faith sat back on the sofa with her mask in place. His grandfather didn't seem to mind. He chatted away about old times while Faith sipped her tea and nodded.

He knew what she'd done—checked into that little place inside her head with its thick, thick walls. He lived out of a similar place himself. But for that soft smile of hers he'd never have guessed those intriguing walls were even there. She hid them well with her on-the-surface frankness and direct words.

She reminded him of Amanda, he realised. Maybe that was why he was reacting so strongly to her. It was another reason he should be doubly wary.

Faith had that same deceptive, ready-for-anything candour that had drawn him to his ex. Remember that word, Marcus. *Deceptive.* Not on purpose, but perhaps that just made the fraud all the more deadly—because it added that hint of honesty that made a man believe in things that just weren't there.

Just as well Faith McKinnon would be off their land and out of their lives before the afternoon was out.

As if she'd read his mind, Faith put down her empty cup. 'Thank you so much for the tea, Bertie,' she said, 'but I have to get going now. I'm renting a cottage down on the coast for the next few weeks.'

'On your own?' His grandfather looked appalled.

Faith nodded. 'It's going to be wonderful.'

It seemed those walls were thicker than even Marcus had guessed.

'I need to go and pick up the keys by three,' Faith said as she collected her bag and other belongings. 'I'll send you the results of my research in a couple of days.'

Bertie raised his eyebrows. 'You might be late picking up those keys,' he said, focusing on the window behind Marcus.

Marcus turned round just as Faith stood up and gasped.

No dusty snow now. Thick feathery flakes were falling hard and fast, so thickly he could hardly see the gatehouse only a hundred feet away.

'I don't think you'll be going anywhere for a while,' his grandfather said, doing his best to look apologetic, but clearly invigorated by the surprise turn in the weather—and events. 'It's far too dangerous to drive in this.'

'What kind of car have you got?' Marcus asked hopefully.

'A Mini.' Faith sighed and took a step closer to the windows. She didn't look as if she believed what she was seeing. 'An old one.'

Well, that was it, then. She'd be hard pressed to make it out of the castle grounds in a car like that, let alone brave the switchback country roads to the motorway.

'It'll probably stop soon,' he said, leaning forward and pressing his nose against the pane. 'Then you can be on your way.'

'In the meantime,' he heard his grandfather say, 'can I interest you in another cup of tea and possibly a toasted crumpet? Shirley makes the most fabulous lemon curd.'

While they drank yet more tea they listened to a weather forecast. Marcus's prediction was soundly contradicted. Heavy snow for the next couple of days. Advice to drive nowhere, anywhere unless it was absolutely necessary.

'Splendid!' Bertie said, clapping his hands. 'We haven't had a good snow in years!'

He was like a big kid again. But then his grandfather had

fond memories of trekking in the Tibetan foothills, and he was going to be able to enjoy this round of snow from the comfort of his fireside chair. Marcus's workload had suddenly doubled, and he was now going to have to tap dance fast to make sure all the Christmas events still went ahead as planned. When had this time of year stopped being fun and started being just another task to be ticked off the list?

He turned away from the window and looked at the other occupant of the yellow drawing room. Faith was back on the sofa again, but this time she wasn't smiling or looking quite so relaxed.

'I can't possibly put you out like this,' she said, looking nervously between grandfather and grandson. 'And I'm used to snow—'

His grandfather straightened in his chair, looking every inch the Duke for once. 'Nonsense! Your grandmother would have my hide if I sent you out in this weather—and, believe me, even after all these years, she is one lady I would not like to get on the wrong side of.'

At the mention of her grandmother Faith's expression changed to one of defeat. 'You have a point there,' she said quietly.

'You can stay here the night and we'll see how the forecast is in the morning.' His grandfather rang the bell at his side again and a few moments later Shirley appeared. 'Miss McKinnon will be staying. Could you make up the turret bedroom?'

'Of course, Your Grace.' Shirley nodded and scurried away.

'But I haven't got any overnight stuff,' Faith said quietly. 'It's all in the back seat of my car.'

Bertie waved a hand. 'Oh, that can be easily sorted. Marcus? Call Parsons on that mobile telephone thing of yours and have someone bring Miss McKinnon's bags in.'

Marcus's eyes narrowed. 'I'll do it,' he almost growled.

His staff had better things to do than to trudge through half a mile of snow with someone's luggage.

'I'll help,' Faith said, standing up.

He shook his head. She'd only complicate matters, and he needed a bit of fresh air and distance from Miss Faith McKinnon.

She frowned, and her body language screamed discomfort. He guessed this didn't sit well with that independent streak of hers. Too bad. At a place like Hadsborough everyone had to work together, like a large extended family. There was no room for loners.

She exhaled. 'In that case the overnight bag in the back will be enough. I don't need the rest.'

'I'll be back shortly,' he said, and exited the room swiftly.

A couple of minutes later he was trudging towards the visitor car park with a scarf knotted round his neck and his collar pulled up. With any luck he'd be repeating this journey in the morning—overnight bag in hand and Faith McKinnon hurrying along behind him.

Faith stood at the turret window that stared out over the lake. A real turret. Like in Rapunzel, her favourite fairy story.

The almost invisible sun was setting behind a wall of soft grey cloud and snowflakes continued to whirl past the mullioned windows, brightening further when they danced close to the panes and caught the glow from the rooms inside. Beyond, the lake was a regal slate-blue, flat as glass, not consenting to be rippled and distorted by the weather. The lawn she'd walked across that morning was now covered in snow—at least a couple of inches already—and bare trees punched through the whiteness as black filigree silhouettes.

How could real people live somewhere so beautiful? It must be a dream.

But the walls seemed solid enough, as did the furniture. Unlike the part of the castle that was open to the public, which was decorated mostly in a medieval style, the rooms in the private wing were more comfortable and modern. They were also filled with antiques and fine furniture, but there was wallpaper on the walls instead of bare stone or tapestries, and there were fitted carpets and central heating. All very elegant.

A smart rap on the door tore her away from the living picture postcard outside her window. She padded across the room in her thick socks and eased the heavy chunk of oak open.

Marcus stood there, fresh flakes of snow half-melted in his hair. Her heart made a painful little bang against her ribcage. *Quit it,* she told it. It had done that all afternoon—every time she caught sight of him.

He was holding her little blue overnight bag. She always packed an emergency bag when she travelled, and it had come in handy more times than she could count when flights had been delayed or travel plans changed. She just hadn't expected to need it in a setting like this.

Or to have a man like this deliver it to her.

He held it out to her and she gripped the padded handles without taking her eyes from his face. He didn't let go. Not straight away. Faith was aware how close their fingers were. It would only take a little twitch and she'd be touching him.

Don't be dumb, Faith. Just because you're staying in a castle for one night it doesn't mean you can live the fairytale. No one's going to climb up to your turret and rescue you. Especially not this man. He'd probably prefer to shove you from it.

She tugged the handles towards her and he let go. A slight expression of surprise lifted his features, as if he'd only just realised he'd hadn't let go when he should have.

'Thank you,' she said, finding her voice hoarse.

'You're welcome,' he replied, but his eyes said she was anything but. 'Dinner is at eight,' he added, glancing at the holdall clenched in her hands. 'We usually change for dinner, but we understand you're at a disadvantage.'

She nodded, not quite sure what to say to that, and Marcus

turned and walked down the long corridor that led to the main staircase. Faith watched him go. Only when he was out of sight did she close the door and dump her bag on the end of the bed.

She unzipped the side pocket, where she always stored her emergency underwear, and then opened the top drawer in an ornate polished wood dresser. Wow. The inside was even lovelier than the outside. Rich, grained walnut, if she wasn't mistaken, with a thick floral lining paper and a silk pouch with dried lavender in it. She took one look at the jumble of bra straps and practical white cotton panties in her hand and dumped them back in her case. Maybe later.

She returned to the window once more.

We usually change for dinner...

A chuckle tickled Faith's lips, but she didn't let it out. *Into what?* she wanted to ask. *Werewolves? Vampires?* Oh, she knew what he meant, but it was another reminder that this was another world. One where people dressed up for dinner and had *luncheon*. Well, she hoped he wasn't expecting ball-gowns or fur stoles from her.

And the tone he'd used... *We understand you're at a disadvantage.*

As if she needed his permission!

In the McKinnon household 'changing for dinner' meant putting your best jeans on—and that was what Faith intended to do.

The brightness behind Faith's lids reminded her of where she was, and why, before she opened her eyes the following morning. She blinked and rolled over to face the window. Snow was piled high on the thin stone ledge. Not good news if she was planning to escape to her little seaside hideaway today.

The bed had been comfy, but she'd had a metaphorical pea under her mattress. Or in her head, to be more accurate—a brooding presence that had been at the fringes of her consciousness all night. As if someone had been looking over her shoulder while she slept.

It was hardly surprising. She'd been aware of his appraising eyes on her all the way through dinner last night, and it had stopped her enjoying what must have been amazing food. Suddenly she'd got all self-conscious about which silver-plated fork to pick up and what she should do with her napkin.

He didn't know what to think of her, did he? Wasn't sure if she was friend or foe.

She'd wanted to jump up and shout, *Neither!* It felt wrong to have been admitted into not only their home but their daily life. *I agree. I shouldn't be here.*

Well, hopefully, if the weather had been kind overnight, she wouldn't be for much longer.

She got out of bed and shuffled over to the window, the comforter wrapped around her, and groaned. It was still snowing hard. Enough for her to know she wasn't going anywhere today, and possibly not tomorrow—not unless the Huntingtons had a snow plough tucked away in one of their garages.

Faith sighed as she watched the scene outside her window. She hadn't seen snow this thick for years—not since she'd last gone home for the Christmas holidays. A little jab of something under her ribcage made her breath catch. Homesickness? Surely not. The bust-ups at Christmas were one of the reasons she'd avoided December in Connecticut ever since.

She glanced at her coat, hanging on the back of the door, remembering how Gram's letter was still stuffed into one of the pockets. She still hadn't read it properly. Now she felt guilty. She stared at her coat. It wasn't that she didn't enjoy Gram's lively and warm narrative, but she knew there was always a price to pay for the pleasure.

Gram's letters always seemed so innocent—full of quirky anecdotes about town life—but in between the news of whose dog had had puppies, complaints about the mayor and Gram's book club gossip was a plea.

Come home.

Faith knew she should, and she planned to some time soon, but she really didn't want to this Christmas. She was too busy, too exhausted. And if both her sisters and her mother turned up there'd be more than enough noise and drama and no one would need Faith there to keep up the numbers. She'd given up trying to be family referee a long time ago, so there was no reason for her to be there.

She walked over to the door and retrieved the crumpled lilac letter. She stared at it for a moment, steeling herself for the inevitable tug on her heartstrings, and then she pulled the pages from the envelope and read.

It was the same old news about the same old town, but it still made her smile.

When she'd finished she reached into her purse and took out the other item that had been in the envelope. Gram had got tired of hinting about her girls coming home and had just gone for the jugular: she'd sent plane tickets to each of the McKinnon sisters, and she'd also requested a 'favour' from each of them. So one sister was travelling from Sydney to Canada, the other had been summoned back to Beckett's Run, and Faith had wound up here, at Hadsborough.

Crafty old woman, Faith thought, frowning. Gram was counting on the fact the sisters wouldn't refuse her—the favour *or* the trip home.

But Faith didn't think she could face it. It would be easier to hide away in her rented cottage until her next job in York. But if she was going to do that she needed time to work up the courage to tell Gram no.

She sighed and pulled yesterday's sweater from her bag. Yesterday's jeans, too. But before she went downstairs she had some internet research to do. Today she was not going to get caught out by Marcus Huntington.

It was still snowing hard when Marcus made the short walk from the estate office in the old stable block back to the castle. He prised his boots from his feet and left them by the kitchen door, then shook the ice off his coat before hanging it on a hook.

He'd almost forgotten about their unexpected guest until he walked into the drawing room and discovered Faith McKinnon sitting on the sofa she'd occupied yesterday. This time, instead of perching on the edge of the seat, she was sitting back against the comfy cushions, her legs crossed, drinking tea out of their Royal Doulton.

When she heard him approach she turned to look at him and put her teacup back on its saucer on the small mahogany table. The warmth that had been in her eyes faded.

'Good morning, Lord Westerham,' she said evenly.

Ah, she'd done her homework, had she? Discovered that as Bertie's heir he had the use of one of his grandfather's lesser titles. Not only that, she'd worked out the proper form of address for a courtesy earl. He wasn't sure if he should be impressed or irritated. It would depend on whether she was trying to be polite or to butter him up. He could accept the former, but he detested the latter, and he didn't know enough about her or her motives to guess which was true.

'I've been talking to the landlord of the Duke's Head in Hadsborough village,' he said, looking at his grandfather. 'He says the snow is drifting and it's already more than a foot deep in some of the lanes.'

'But the snow ploughs will be here soon, right?' Faith stopped abruptly, as if she hadn't meant to blurt that out.

He gave a rueful smile. 'Oh, they'll be here—eventually.'

'And by "eventually" you mean…?'

Bertie reached over and patted her arm. 'They'll concentrate on the motorways and the main roads first,' he said. 'We don't get much traffic in this neck of the woods. But don't you worry… They'll be here in a few days.'

'That's crazy! At home in Beckett's Run the roads would be clear by the next morning.'

Marcus stepped forward. 'Unfortunately this isn't Beckett's Run.'

She looked up at him, the look on her face telling him she was all too clear on that point. He met her gaze—the challenge she gave without even opening her mouth. And that was when it happened again. That strange feeling of everything swirling round them coming to rest. And this time they hadn't even been touching.

Faith was sitting stock still, her face deadpan, but he saw the flash of panic in her eyes before the shutters came down.

'Sorry, my dear,' his grandfather said, looking less than crestfallen at the prospect of having an unexpected house guest. 'It seems as if you're stuck with us for a while yet.'

Faith tore her gaze from Marcus's and fixed them on Bertie. 'In that case,' she said, in a very brisk and business-like fashion, 'is there somewhere I can plug my laptop in? I might as well get on with that research.'

She was meticulous. He'd give her that. Marcus watched as Faith wrote carefully in a large notebook with a pencil. She'd been at it since he'd returned just after lunch, pulling up research on her laptop and then recording it in her notebook in a clear, neat hand. He had the feeling she wasn't the kind to scribble away furiously, no matter how excited she got.

He looked out of the window. The low sun was a pale glowing disc in a gunmetal sky. It had been snowing too hard most of the day for their guest to venture to the chapel, but now the weather had lost its fervour and flakes drifted lazily towards the ground. The forecasts had predicted clear skies tomorrow. He hoped they were right.

'Haven't you got other things you need to do?' Faith asked quietly as she reached for the mouse once again.

He shook his head, and noted the glimmer of irritation that flashed across her features.

'Are you sure?'

She didn't like him hanging around watching her? Too bad. This was his family—his life she was carefully digging into before pulling it apart bit by bit—and today at least he had the luxury of being able to witness each new discovery. He needed to know before his grandfather if she unearthed anything significant.

'You know what? If you're so interested in what I'm doing—' and the look on her face said she didn't believe that for a second '—it would really help if you could check the estate archives for any mention of the window.'

'I already have.'

She raised her eyebrows hopefully but he shook his head.

'You're sure? Finding some documentary evidence one way or the other would help me finish this more quickly.'

The eyebrows lifted again, but this time they had a slightly knowing air. She knew he'd like that suggestion.

He was ashamed to admit it was true. Something about her straightforward 'don't care' attitude set his hair on end and raised his awareness.

He didn't have the luxury of not caring. Once, maybe, he'd thought he'd be able to forge his own path, create his own life, but his father's actions had scuppered those fantasies nicely. Now he had to care, whether he wanted to or not, and it irritated him that he'd been confronted with someone who had perfected that skill so perfectly.

He glanced over at her again. Her dark ponytail hung forward, draping over her shoulder, and she was lost in concentration. It didn't stop him admiring the thick, slightly wavy hair, or her small, fine features.

No, not that kind of awareness, Marcus.

Well, partly that.

Okay, he found her attractive. But that wasn't what he

meant. Ever since she'd arrived and sent Bertie into hyper-drive about this window he'd felt like one of those big black guard dogs the security team used.

He'd spent two years trying to rebuild the family name after the crash of his father's investment company and sub-sequent death, and now he'd discovered he couldn't stand himself down when a potential threat appeared.

The current threat was crouched over her laptop on the an-tique desk, and he had no business noticing its thick ponytail or elegant nose. He didn't want her digging around in the fam-ily's past. Any skeletons lurking around in the Huntingdon closet—and he was sure there were many—should remain undiscovered. Maybe not for ever, but for now. He didn't want to hide from the truth—just to wait until things were more settled.

As for his out-of-leftfield attraction to Faith McKinnon? He sighed. Well, maybe he didn't need to worry about that. The fact that he'd 'changed' after his father's death was one of the things that had sent Amanda running. She'd told him she was fed up with his snapping and snarling. Apparently women didn't find it very appealing. And from the looks Faith McKinnon had been giving him all afternoon she'd joined that lengthy queue. Even if there was something strange hum-ming between them, he was pretty certain she wasn't going to act on it.

And neither was he. So that was all good.

'Oh, my…'

Something about the tone of Faith's breathy exclamation stopped him short. He leaned forward to look at the laptop screen. She was transfixed by an image of an oil painting of a richly robed redhead in a beautiful garden, her arms over-flowing with fruit.

'That looks a bit like the window,' he said.

Faith looked up at him, her eyes shining. 'It looks *a lot* like the window! Do you see that plant with yellow flowers in the corner?' She used the mouse to zoom in on one section of the high-res photo, showing a low-lying bush. 'It's quite distinctive,' she said, indicating the papery leaves and, in the centre of each bloom, an explosion of long yellow filaments with red tips.

Marcus blinked. He was having trouble concentrating on what she was saying. That shine in her eyes had momentarily distracted him. All day she'd been like a robot, hardly talking to him, interacting as little as possible, and all of a sudden she was zinging with energy.

He cleared his throat. 'And this means something?'

'Maybe!' She ran her hand over her smoothed-back hair and stood up, let out a little bemused laugh. 'I don't know…' Her face fell. 'Darn! I forgot to take a photo of the window when we were in the chapel yesterday.' She shook her head, excitement turning to frustration, then marched over to the window to inspect the weather. 'It's not snowing nearly as hard now. Do you think we could go back? I need to see it up close—compare the two side by side.'

Marcus was so taken with this moving, talking Faith that he forgot to question if he should be pleased about this new discovery or not. 'I don't see why not.'

She was almost out through the door before he'd finished speaking, running to get her coat and boots. He followed her out of the drawing room, only to be almost bowled over when she dashed back to pick up her laptop.

'Come on,' she said, the hint of a smile tugging at the corners of her mouth. 'It'll be dark soon and I want to find out for sure.'

He nodded, not quite sure what else he could say, and then he wrapped up warm and followed Faith McKinnon out into the snow.

Marcus stood back, arms folded, as Faith walked close to the window, her laptop balanced on her upturned hands. She looked from screen to window and back again repeatedly, and then she sat down on the end of the nearest pew and stared straight ahead.

He went and sat beside her. Not too close. She didn't register his presence.

'Are you okay?' His low voice seemed to boom in the empty chapel.

Faith kept looking straight ahead and nodded dreamily. Marcus was just starting to wonder if he should call somebody when she turned to him and gave him the brightest, most beautiful smile he'd ever seen. It was as if up until that moment Faith McKinnon had been broadcasting in black and white and she'd suddenly switched to colour.

'You've found something?' he said.

She nodded again, but this time her head bobbed rapidly and her smile brightened further. 'I think this window might be Samuel Crowbridge's work after all!'

Ah. That. Marcus breathed out. Nothing about a message, then. Good.

She twisted the laptop his way, showing him the zoomed-in picture of the little bunch of yellow flowers. 'They're identical,' she said triumphantly, 'and rather stylised. Rose of Sharon, the article says—although they look nothing like the ones in my grandmother's garden. Anyway, the chances of two different artists representing them this way is highly unlikely.'

He frowned. 'I thought you said Crowbridge had moved on from that style.'

A quick flick of her fingers over the mousepad and he was looking at the full picture once again.

'I know,' she said, 'but I think I may have found the reason he returned to it.' She clicked again and now a webpage appeared, dense with text. The painting was now a long rectangle down one side. 'Crowbridge was commissioned to do three paintings for a rather wealthy patron in the 1850s—

Faith, Hope and Charity—but only completed two out of the three before his patron changed his mind.'

Her lips curved into the most bewitching smile, and he couldn't help but focus on her lips as she continued to explain.

'Apparently they were modelled on his wife and two mistresses, and mistress number two fell out of favour.'

His eyebrows rose a notch, and he found his own lips starting to curve. 'You don't say?' He glanced back at the screen.

'Both paintings have been in a private collection for a long time—hardly ever seen, let alone photographed—but one recently went to auction.' She paused and her lips twitched a little. 'The original...*inspiration* for the trio of paintings came to light, and the family—understandably—decided to part with the picture that *wasn't* of Great-Great-Grandma.'

He nodded at the screen. 'Which virtue is she?'

'Charity,' she said firmly, and then her gaze drifted to the stained glass. 'Oh, how I wish there was a photo of the other one...'

She stood up, set the laptop down on the pew in front and walked over to the window.

Even in the dull light of a winter's afternoon the stained glass picture was beautiful. The pale sun, now on its way to setting, gently warmed the outside of the glass. As Faith drew near patches of pastel colour fell on her face, highlighting her cheekbones. Drawn like a magnet, he stood and walked towards her.

His throat seemed to be full of gravel. He swallowed a couple of times to dislodge it. 'And how does that relate to our window?'

No. Not *our*. At least not in the way he'd meant it when he'd said it. It should be his and Bertie's *our,* not his and Faith's *our.*

He was standing opposite her, with the window on his right, and she turned to face him. The patchwork colours of the window fell on one side of their faces, marking them identically.

'I'm not sure,' she said, and closed her eyes for the briefest of moments, almost as if she was sending up a silent prayer.

Marcus took another step forward.

She opened her eyes and looked at him. Right into him.

'I think Crowbridge may have taken the chance, years later, to finish his trilogy. But not in oils this time—in stained glass.'

'I see.' He looked back, not breaking eye contact, amazed that he could see layer upon layer of things deep in those eyes that had previously been shuttered. 'So this one here would be…?'

'Faith,' she whispered.

No longer did their words seem to echo. They were absorbed by the thick air surrounding the pair of them. Her eyes widened slightly and a soft breath escaped her lips.

Faith. The word reverberated inside his head. But he wasn't looking at the window. In fact he'd forgotten all about it. His gaze moved from her eyes to her nose, and then lower…

'Yes,' he said softly, leaning dangerously closer.

CHAPTER FOUR

SOMEONE was playing drums somewhere. Loudly. They were echoing in Faith's ears.

'Uh—' Her lips parted of their own accord.

Stop it, she shouted to herself silently. *What on earth do you think you're doing? You know this is a really bad idea, and you're not some brainless bimbo who can't think straight when an attractive man is around. At least you've never been up until now.*

Thankfully Marcus came to his senses first, although something inside Faith ripped like Velcro when he abruptly stepped back and turned his focus once again to the kneeling woman in the window, beautiful and serene.

What had happened just then? She blinked a couple of times. Marcus was scowling at her, as usual, and it was as if the last couple of minutes hadn't happened. She folded her arms across her chest and scowled back.

A muscle at the side of his jaw twitched. 'What does this mean? For us?'

Faith's heart stopped. 'For *us?*' she repeated in a whisper.

'For the family,' he said, very matter-of-factly. 'For the Huntingtons.'

Oh, for *them*. Not her. He hadn't been including her. Not that she'd expected him to, of course. Or wanted him to.

'I don't know. Before I can say anything definitive I'll

have to investigate further.' She swallowed. 'I'd need your consent for that.'

He didn't say anything. And he was looking less than impressed at the idea of her poking around his family's home and history.

He was going to say no, wasn't he? She could see it in his face. He was going to tell his grandfather it was too much trouble, too much inconvenience—to protect that lovely old man from the 'upset', as he put it. A flash of anger detonated inside her. Her older sister liked to boss people around that way, make their decisions for them. That kind of behaviour had always driven her crazy. She wasn't going to back down. She didn't care what he thought. The world had a right to know if this was Crowbridge's window.

'There's some minor damage in the corner, and what repair attempts have been made are very poor. If this window turns out to be what I think it might be I could restore it for you. Free of charge. Payment in kind for letting me investigate further. If I'm right, the PR value for the castle—and your family—would be great. And more publicity means more visitors.'

Then she laid down her ace. 'And, of course, your grandfather would know beyond a shadow of a doubt that every inch of the window has been investigated and documented.' She breathed in quickly. 'I'm stuck here for at least a couple of days anyway, and you said you wanted something concrete for Bertie. Well, this kind of work would be about as concrete as you could get.'

He folded his arms. 'What would this *research* involve?'

He said it as if it was a dirty word. Faith's spine straightened. Any beginnings of the truce they'd been beginning to build were gone. Obviously ripped away when he'd had what must have been a *What were you thinking?* moment in the split second before his lips had come close to hers. Just like that they were on opposite sides of the battlefield again.

She lifted her chin, even though inside she was cringing. Why couldn't it have been her who'd pulled away? Now she just felt pathetic and rejected and he had the moral high ground. Of *course* he wouldn't go around kissing an ordinary girl like her. She should have known that. Should have backed off first. But she'd been too excited about the window to care...

Well, she was still excited about the window.

Only now she'd gained a much-needed sense of perspective, too. Good. She'd needed that. Thank you, Marcus Huntington, Earl Westerham, and future eighth Duke of Hadsborough. He had actually done her a favour.

It didn't mean she was going to curtsey or anything.

'Faith tells me she's offered to repair the window free,' his grandfather said over dinner that evening.

Not free, Marcus thought. There was a price. It just didn't involve money.

He picked up his soup spoon. 'Surely proper research will take more than the couple of days you'll be stuck here?' he asked.

A little bit of her bread roll seemed to get stuck in her throat. 'A couple of days will tell me if it's worth pursuing,' she said hoarsely. 'Then, if you give me the go-ahead to repair, I guess it'd take a couple of weeks. I'd finish in time for the Carol Service, I promise you. And I won't intrude on your hospitality any further once the roads are clear. I can commute from the cottage in Whitstable.'

His grandfather made a dismissive noise, letting them know what he thought about that. 'Nonsense. You'll stay here. It's a complete waste of time and petrol to do otherwise.'

Faith opened her mouth and closed it again. Marcus could tell from the determined look on her face she wasn't happy with that idea, but she was sensible enough to leave that battle for another day. There was no talking to his grandfather when he remembered he was a duke after all, and started issuing orders.

It was clear the old man wasn't about to have anyone spoil his fun, and he seemed quite taken with their unexpected guest.

And so are you, seeing as you almost kissed her in the chapel.

Ah, but he'd stopped himself in time. And just as well. Because he wasn't going to choose with his heart again. Love was a see-saw, and Marcus was going to make damn sure he ended up high in the air next time. He would be the one who held the power and could walk away if he wanted to. He'd do what his family had done for generations—choose a sensible girl from a suitable family who would bring some stability and support to the Huntington line.

It was just hard to remember that when Faith McKinnon fixed him with those dark brown eyes of hers and stared at him, peeling him layer by layer, making him feel she could see right inside him. Worse still, he could feel his reluctance to push her away growing. And that was dangerous. Without those walls of his in place he was likely to do something stupid. They were all that stopped him repeating the whole Amanda fiasco.

He reached for the pepper and ground a liberal amount on his soup. 'So you're saying that this research of yours won't disrupt us?'

Her chin tipped up a notch and she looked him in the eye. 'Less than the snow. I promise you that.'

Touché.

While he didn't appreciate her defiance, he admired her pluck. Not many people challenged him outright on anything these days.

'Are you going to take the window away?' his grandfather asked, echoing what Marcus had been hoping.

Faith shook her head. 'I need to be close to the whole window to do my research—not just the bit of it I'm repairing. But I own most of the equipment I'd need, and I can order in supplies quite easily when the snow clears. The first phase will be observation and documentation anyway.' She shot him a hopeful glance. 'I was wondering if you had a space where I can work on the bottom pane? I'd only need a room with a trestle table and decent light.'

Marcus's shoulders stiffened. Unfortunately they had the perfect spot.

Bertie knew it, too. He grinned. 'Of course. Then what?'

'Then I'll snip the old lead away and clean the glass before putting it back together.'

Bertie nodded seriously. 'You will keep your eyes peeled, won't you? For anything unusual?'

She swallowed and glanced quickly at Marcus. He shot her a warning look. She lowered her eyelids slightly at him, before turning her attention back to his grandfather and acting as if their little exchange had never happened.

'Of course I will investigate every area of the window carefully,' she said, her voice losing its characteristic briskness, 'but none of the usual rules apply, and I haven't seen writing of any kind.'

Bertie's face fell. He folded his napkin and placed it on the table.

She reached over and covered her hand with his. 'I promise I will try to keep an open mind,' she added, 'but only if you promise to do the same.'

He nodded, and then smiled at her gently. 'Thank you, Faith. If anyone can unravel this secret it will be you.'

She withdrew her hand and sat back in her chair. 'I'll do my best, Bertie,' she said, shaking her head, 'but you have to face the possibility that what you're looking for may not be there.'

'Holy cow!' Faith said.

'Quite,' was Marcus's dry response.

She'd never seen so much junk in her life. She'd thought Gram's attic was bad. But Gram and Grandpa had only lived in their house fifty years. The Huntingtons had lived at Hadsborough for more than four hundred, and it seemed that no one had ever, *ever* thrown anything away. They'd just stuffed it in the unused vaults under the castle.

They both stood in the doorway and just stared.

Marcus, who had been holding the door open, nudged a little doorstop under it with his foot and walked a couple of paces into the room.

A retired servant, whose sons still worked for the estate, had tipped Marcus off about this place. There had to be at least a couple of centuries worth of debris here, so they were sure to stumble upon something to help her.

She needed to find something that would link Samuel Crowbridge to this window. If she announced her suspicions to the academic community without proof someone could hijack it, find the evidence she lacked, and it wouldn't be her find any more.

'Let's get started, shall we?' she said wearily.

The rooms weren't totally below ground, but with snow piled high against the long, horizontal windows just below the ceiling they might as well have been.

'I was told the cellar wasn't in use,' Marcus said.

'It isn't,' she replied. 'By the looks of it the last of the junk was stuffed in here at least a decade ago.'

His eyebrows rose as the said the word *junk*.

'You know what I mean.'

He strolled over to an old, but definitely not antique filing cabinet and peered inside the bottom drawer. The rusty runners squeaked painfully as he pushed it closed again.

'Stuffed badger,' he said, a faint air of bemusement about him.

'A real one?'

He nodded.

She walked over to the filing cabinet to take a look for herself. It wasn't a very big one, but sure enough a ratty-looking stuffed animal with glass eyes sat morosely at the bottom of the deep drawer, staring at the painted metal sides. She did as Marcus had done and shut the drawer, then she turned to look at him and said, quite seriously, 'Of course it is. That's where I keep mine—amongst the filing. You never know when it's going to come in handy.'

That earned her a smile. Sort of.

Good. If she could get him to lighten up a bit it might help her sanity. For some reason he was on red alert around her, and she sensed it was more than just her intrusion into his family. She had the feeling she was his own personal brand of dynamite.

Which means he should handle you with care...

She slapped the masochistic part of herself that had come up with that dumb thought. He wasn't going to be *handling* her anywhere. At all. Ever. She needed to get that into her thick skull.

Which was easier said than done. Especially as the more he glowered at her the more her pulse skipped. What was wrong with her? Really? Why did something inside her whisper that she should stop running in the opposite direction and just give in?

And when she was aware of him watching her—which was always—her skin tingled and her concentration vanished. She did her best to ignore the prickling sensation up her spine when he was near, but it seemed to be getting stronger all the time.

There it went again—like a pair of fingers walking up her back.

She decided to search the other side of the room from him, just to see if a little extra distance would help.

It didn't.

'Do you think there's any order to this stuff?' she called

out as she lifted the top ledger in a dusty pile and inspected the front page: *Meat ordering: 1962-65.* Fascinating for the right person, probably, but not what she was looking for. She put it down again and inspected the rest of the stack. They were various household accounts from the fifties and sixties—all decades too late to help her.

'We could spend weeks searching this place,' she said as she came across Marcus again behind a stack of crates. 'Just rummaging could be pointless. What we really need to do is sort it all out, clean the room and put it in some order.'

He nodded. 'But you're supposed to be working on the window. You haven't got time to clean my cellar for me.'

Ah, the ticking clock inside his head—counting down to the moment when she would leave. Even now it made itself apparent.

She nodded up to the snow packed against the windows. After a brief reprieve the snow had returned with a vengeance. 'At the moment I can't even get to the chapel, and I need to find some documentary back-up,' she replied. 'I'm stuck here twenty-four-seven and you haven't got cable. What else am I going to do with my time?'

Marcus just shook his head and wandered off, muttering something about the sheer stupidity of trying to lay cable in a moat and how satellite dishes would spoil the roofline. Faith let her mouth twitch. This getting Marcus to lighten up thing was almost fun, and it had the added bonus that if she managed to keep him from glowering at her she might start acting sensibly for a change.

He was saved from answering her by a rap on the open cellar door. A man she didn't recognise poked his head in, and he and Marcus talked in hushed voices. Faith decided not to eavesdrop and took herself to the far side of the cellar and leafed through a stack of old papers. He reappeared a couple of minutes later, looking frustrated.

'Problems?' Faith asked.

He huffed. 'Nothing to do with the window. We host a Christmas Ball every year and ticket sales have ground to a halt. My events manager says the forecast for ongoing snow is to blame.'

'When is it?'

'A week on Saturday.' A grimace of annoyance passed across his features. 'I really don't want to cancel it. We've already laid out a lot of money, and no ball means no revenue and plenty of lost deposits.'

'But you can cover that, right? It's not like you'll be going without your Christmas lunch because of it.'

He gave her a look that told her she didn't know much about anything. 'A place like this *eats* money,' he said carefully. 'I know it might not look like it from the outside, but even Hadsborough feels the pinch of tough economic times.' He shook his head. 'People are worried about getting stuck on the motorway in the snow, or stranded at the station if trains get cancelled.'

She picked up a dusty newspaper and looked at it. 'Can't they just put on some snowboots and walk?'

'Most of the guests aren't local. The ball is a very exclusive event, and people come from all over the south of England.'

He mentioned a ticket price that made her eyes water.

'No wonder people are wary about spending that much and then not even getting here.' She replaced the newspaper on its pile. 'You know what? You should drop the ticket price and get the locals to come—have a party for the villagers. I know it won't raise as much money, but there's a whole heap of other stuff you could do quite cheaply—'

Marcus stood up ramrod-straight. 'Miss McKinnon, I'm very grateful for your…input…but my family has been running this estate for three hundred years. Maybe you should concentrate your opinions on your own area of expertise.'

She blinked. Well, that told *her,* didn't it?

But she found she wasn't going to sigh and ignore it, as

she would have done if one of her sisters had delivered such a stinging put-down. She found she couldn't just walk away from Marcus Huntington when he issued a challenge.

'Actually, when it comes to Christmas I'm something of an expert.'

His face was deadpan. 'You do surprise me. I hadn't pegged you as the reindeer jumper and flashing Santa earrings type.'

'Well, I didn't reckon you'd be quite so up your own butt when I first met you, but it seems you're not the only one who can be wrong.'

His expression was thunderous for a moment, but all of a sudden he threw back his head and laughed. It was a rich, earthy sound, most unlike his clipped speaking voice, and it made him seem like a completely different man. Faith wasn't sure if she wanted to march over there and slap him, or if she should just let go of the tension in her jaw and join him.

'I'm sorry,' he said, when he'd finally regained his composure. 'You're right. I was being horrendously pompous.' And then he spoilt his apology by bursting out laughing again. He dragged his hand over his eyes then looked at her. 'You're very direct, aren't you?'

This time Faith joined him. Just a little chuckle. It was hard not to when she saw the warmth in those normally intense blue eyes.

'So where does all this Christmas expertise come from?' he asked.

'I grew up in a small town that takes the holidays *very* seriously,' she replied. 'Anything that's fixed down—and a few things that aren't—are in danger of being draped with fairy lights and tinsel during the week-long festival each year, running up to Christmas Eve.' She shook her head gently, smiling. 'I pretended I hated it when I was a teenager.' The smile faded away. 'I suppose I kinda miss it.'

Wow. She hadn't expected those words to come out of her

mouth. She suddenly remembered those plane tickets burning a hole in her purse upstairs in the turret.

'When were you last home for Christmas?' he asked.

'Five years ago.'

That was a long time, wasn't it? Suddenly a pang of something hot speared her deep inside. She brushed it away. She didn't *do* homesickness. It was probably something to do with the fact that Marcus had stepped closer, and the fact that he'd stopped glaring at her and was looking down at her with a mixture of understanding and curiosity. Which meant it was her cue to step away.

'Anyway,' she said brightly, shuffling backwards, 'I'm sure there's something you could do here that wouldn't cost the earth and would generate some income.'

Marcus gave her another one of his dry half-smiles. 'As long as it doesn't involve putting a light-up Santa and sleigh on the castle roof I'll keep an open mind.'

She nodded. 'Good. Now, where do you think is the best place to start sorting through this junk?'

'Please, Faith,' he said, but the smile didn't fade completely, making her feel like a co-conspirator rather than an adversary, 'this isn't all junk—some of it is history.'

He'd called her Faith instead of Miss McKinnon. Wonders would never cease.

She smiled. 'Okay… Which bits of this *history* do you think we should put in a garbage sack first?'

Marcus started to open his mouth.

'Kidding!' she added quickly. 'Really, you are too easy sometimes.'

Marcus shook his head and turned away to investigate a pile of tattered copies of *Punch!* Even though his back was turned she could sense he was closer to smiling instead of scowling—which made things more comfortable on quite a few fronts—and they worked side by side for the next half an hour in something approaching comfortable silence.

Then Marcus checked his watch and showed her the time. 'Not long until dinner,' he said.

They both straightened, dusted themselves off and looked at each other.

Clunk. It happened again. That feeling of coming to rest, slotting in. Faith held her breath.

'And we'll carry on tomorrow?' she asked, letting the air out in one go.

He nodded. 'It depends what the weather does, but I can't see those supplies you ordered getting through for another couple of days at least.'

'In that case I have one request,' she said.

Marcus's brows drew together. He didn't much like being told what to do, did he? Didn't like being indebted to anyone in any way. The humour drained from his face, and once again she was reminded of a sleek hunting animal.

The easy banter they'd shared for a few minutes had lulled her into a sense of false security—made her think she could make him less of a threat. She'd been wrong. Just ask its prey how tame the hound was; it knew the wildness that lay underneath the groomed and elegant coat. It didn't attempt to befriend it; it took one look and ran. A lesson she should not forget.

She folded her arms across her chest. 'The badger stays,' she said, doing her best to appear composed and in control under his gaze. It would be a good reminder for her every time she was tempted to do something dumb. A stuffed and glassy-eyed chaperone. One that obviously hadn't run when it should have done.

The intensity of his gaze didn't waver, but his lips curved into a grudging smile and he nodded.

Unfortunately his change of expression didn't help matters one bit. Faith felt that smile down to her toes. Nope. Not safe at all, that smile.

As he opened the filing cabinet drawer and lifted the badger out she drew in a shaky breath.

She needed help. Big time. Because if he kept looking at her like that the woman in Bertie's window wouldn't be the only one on her knees asking for heavenly assistance. Faith would be right there beside her.

CHAPTER FIVE

ONCE again Faith was following Marcus across the castle lawn and off the island. This time, however, their footsteps left six-inch deep impressions in the flawless snow. Here, near the lake, it wasn't that deep, but Marcus had told her it had drifted quite high in some of the dips and dells on the estate.

Out on the road to the main gate a tractor was spreading grit, and up near the old stables a team of men with snow shovels were clearing the paths.

Faith peeked from under the brim of her knitted hat and cast her eyes upwards as her breath made little icy clouds. The sky was the most amazing blend of the palest pastels, from rose-petal pink at the horizon through lilac and lavender to crisp blue high above.

As she walked along a wide path that led away from the castle she could see that the water from the lake flowed underneath their feet and filled a second lake, longer and thinner. On the far side were fields and pockets of woodland, but she couldn't see the nearest bank as it curved round the low hill where the stable block was situated.

In front of the stables the path forked. Faith prepared to leave Marcus, who was on his way to the estate office, and continue her journey to the chapel, but he stopped where the paths divided. 'I'd like to show you something.'

Not exactly a request, but it wasn't an order either. Yesterday she would have said *no way,* suspecting he had a pair of stocks waiting for the interloper, but she couldn't quite wipe the memory of his unguarded laughter from the evening before, so she nodded and followed him under the arch of the redbrick building and into the yard beyond. Single-storey buildings framed the edges of a large cobbled square. Marcus led her to one on the right, unlocked the door and ushered her inside into a large bright space.

'My mother had a fixation with watercolour painting for a while,' he said. 'We had this converted for her.'

Faith took a few steps into the airy studio and stopped. *Wow.* What a view.

The wall opposite the door was all glass, with a stupendous view of the lake. Just outside was a small decked area, and then the land fell away. Beautifully kept terraced gardens, the shape now muffled with great dollops of snow, had been cut into the side of the hill as it dipped towards the lake. Geese floated aimlessly on the water and she watched silently as a low-flying swan made a rather inelegant landing, carving a wake on the lake's surface and causing the other birds to flutter and scurry.

'Will this do for a workspace?'

She looked back at him. Some people would have described his face as blank, but Faith knew better. She could see a difference in his eyes, in the set of his mouth. She knew instantly what this meant. This was his way of calling a truce.

Nothing as simple as a laying down of arms, though. Marcus was like those medieval castles that had rings and rings of walls and defences, and she understood that all he'd done was let her inside the first gate.

And she was quite happy to camp for the remainder of her time at Hadsborough. One notch down from frosty resentment suited her just fine. She'd be safe from those sizzling glares, but not close enough to be tempted by what she saw inside. This would be good. She could handle cordial but distant Marcus.

'So this space will work for you?' he said.

'Yes, thank you,' she replied, giving her best impression of calm and professional. *Fake it,* she told herself. *Pretty soon the rest of you will catch up and it'll become real.*

If only she'd known just how wrong she was—just how the glimmer of humour in his eyes would be her undoing.

'I'm sure you'd tell me if it didn't,' he said.

Faith blinked. Was Marcus—was *the Earl*—teasing her?

The jittery feeling she'd been fighting fairly successfully since the night before returned, but she lifted her chin and looked at him while she locked everything down. Made sure not a hint of a tremor showed on the outside.

'You got that right,' she said, and then she turned and headed back towards the door—away from the beautiful view, away from the beautiful man. Sensible gal.

'Now, I'm off to see that window before we both freeze our butts off.'

She ignored the huff of dry laughter behind her and headed back out into the cold, hoping the chilly air would rob her cheeks of some of their colour.

'That's you? Standing on top of the Great Pyramid?' Faith bent over Bertie's old photo album on the coffee table in front of the fire. Her dark hair swung forward, obscuring her face.

The old man nodded and smiled the smile that she only saw when he was sharing his photo albums with her. One with a tinge of recklessness.

'They used to let you do that in those days.'

'You've been to so many wonderful places,' she said, turning the page and finding more of Bertie and his wife, Clara, in exotic locations. 'My youngest sister likes to travel. Gram says she never could sit still as a child either.'

'Me, too,' Bertie said, sighing and relaxing back into his

wing-backed chair. 'Still wouldn't if I had the choice. Only do it now because I've got to.'

She nodded in mock seriousness. 'But still an adventurer on the inside,'

There was that smile again—the one born of memories of exploration and exploits. 'You betcha, as your grandma used to say.'

Faith's eyes grew wide. 'She did *not!*' Gram had always been a stickler for proper diction and polite manners.

She'd been here five days now. Her preliminary observation and documentation of the window was complete, and tomorrow she would move the bottom of the section to the studio, where she could begin the painstaking work of removing all the old lead, gently cleaning the antique glass and putting it all back together again.

Five days? Had it only been that long? She and Bertie were already firm friends, and she looked forward to their after-dinner chats, when he would regale her with stories from his travels. From the occasional hoist of Marcus's eyebrows as he sat in the other armchair, reading a thriller, she guessed some of the details had become more and more embellished as the years had gone by, but she didn't mind.

'My Lord?' Shirley appeared at the door. 'Telephone call for you.'

Marcus nodded and stood up, excusing himself.

The grandson? Well, he was another kettle of fish. Bertie had welcomed her warmly into his home, but she was still camped inside that first gate of Marcus's defences. She reminded herself that was just what she wanted. Even if it was more like walking a tightrope than camping somewhere safe, at least she *was* walking it. Just.

Marcus returned from his phone call and took up his customary place in the armchair opposite his grandfather. He crossed his legs and picked up his book. 'Parsons says they finished clearing the lanes of snow today. You're free,' he added, with a nod in Faith's direction, 'should you want to fly.'

'Ridiculous,' Bertie said in a dismissive tone. 'I've told you what your grandmother will do to me if I toss you out. You're staying here and that's that.' He closed his newspaper as if that was the end of the subject. 'My grandson tells me you've been badgering him with ideas for the Christmas Ball,' he said, moving on to another topic of conversation.

Faith knew it was useless to argue, so she went with the flow. 'I've suggested lowering the ticket price, relaxing the dress code and inviting people from the village. You wouldn't have to cancel if you did that.'

Marcus looked at her over the top of his paperback. 'The number of people from Hadsborough village who have attended the ball in the past has been very small. I don't think they're interested.'

'I mean something more accessible than an over-priced event that only a handful of rich outsiders can afford. I grew up in a small town, so I understand the mentality. Get them all involved, make them feel it's *their* party, too, and they might just surprise you. Tickets would sell like hot cakes. They must be proud of the castle, of being linked with it—I know I would be if I lived here—so let them show it.'

The grim line of Marcus's mouth told her he wasn't convinced.

Faith shrugged. 'Or you could keep going with your idea and lose money hand over fist. Up to you.'

Bertie chuckled and clapped his hands together. 'She's got you there, my boy!'

Marcus didn't answer straight away. 'I'll think about it,' he muttered, and he picked up his book and obscured his face with it once more.

Marcus whistled as he closed the estate office door behind him. He checked his watch. Four-fifteen. The sun would be setting soon, and he could already feel the impatient frost sharpening the air. It had snowed again over the last couple of days, as the forecast had predicted, but not as hard as it had when Faith had first got here.

Still, on top of the previous snow some of the surrounding lanes were once again blocked, complicating matters. Thank goodness they'd had a couple of clear days that had allowed for deliveries—including Faith's supplies for the window restoration.

He crossed the courtyard and headed for the studio door. After a busy day at the estate office, dealing with all the extra work the weather had thrown up, he'd got into the habit of checking up on Faith near the end of the working day.

When the natural light began to fade she'd sit up from being hunched over the stained glass panel and rub her eyes, as if she was waking from a long and drowsy sleep. Tenacious wasn't the word. If he caught her at just the right time he'd see the warm, vibrant Faith who'd visited the other day in the chapel—the one who only came to life when she was talking about or working on the window.

He knew he probably shouldn't want to catch a glimpse of this other Faith, but she didn't hang around for long. Once the tools were back in their box she disappeared, and temptation was safely out of reach. It wasn't wrong to just *look,* was it? It wasn't as if he was going to do something stupid and *touch.*

He knocked on the door to warn her of his approach, and then opened it without waiting for an answer. He found her just as he'd expected to—perched on a stool next to the trestle table, spine curved forward as she snipped the soft lead away from the antique glass with a pair of cutters.

When she heard his footsteps she put her tools down and then linked her hands above her head in a stretch that elongated her spine. Marcus stopped where he was, suddenly transfixed by the slight swaying movement as she stretched the muscles on first one side of her torso and then the other.

That motion was doing a fabulous job of emphasising her slender waist through her grey polo neck jumper.

Forget stockings and corsets. It seemed that softly clinging knitwear was enough to do it for him these days. Had he been without significant female company for too long? Or was this just a sign that he was getting old, and cardigans and suchlike were going to float his boat from now on? Either way he answered that question it was a pretty sad state of affairs.

Faith stopped stretching and turned round to talk to him, which—thankfully—gave Marcus the use of his vocal cords once again.

'Is it that time already?' She pushed up a sleeve and checked her watch, frowned slightly at it, then got up to head off to the large window that filled the opposite wall. The setting sun was hidden by the castle, but it had turned the lake below them shades of rich pink and tangerine. She sighed as he walked across the space to join her.

'Ready?' he said.

She turned towards him and nodded. 'Sure.'

This, too, had become a habit. Just as his feet had fallen into taking him to the studio at the end of the day, he and Faith had fallen into a routine of meeting up and going down to the cellar when the working day was over. After more than a week of evenings dusting and sorting and tidying they'd made progress.

He knew he could have snapped his fingers and had a whole crew descend on the place and sort it out in a matter of days, but he was quite enjoying sifting through the debris of earlier generations bit by bit. A couple of hours of quiet each evening before dinner, when he was free to do something that interested him rather than something that *had* to be done, was doing him good.

She collected her things, put her coat on and looped a scarf around her neck, before turning the light off and shutting the door. Marcus pulled the key from his pocket and locked it behind them, then they strolled back down the hill towards the castle, its silhouette dark against the sunset.

She filled him in on her progress with the window.

'It's strange,' she said, and frowned. 'It's obvious the bottom of the window has been repaired before. Quite soon after its installation, if I'm right about the age of the materials. I wonder what happened to it.'

He made a noncommittal kind of face. 'Perhaps we'll find an answer if we ever find some purchase records. Someone must have been paid to do the work.'

She nodded thoughtfully. 'Let's hope.'

They made their way down to the cellar and resumed their clear-out operation. Some of the ratty office furniture, which had obviously been dumped here a decade or two ago, when the estate offices had moved to the renovated stable block, had been cleared out, which left them with a little more space. A pile of sturdy lidded plastic crates stood near the door, and anything that might be useful was put safely inside, away from the dust.

They'd also found a lot of 'garbage', as Faith called it, a few treasures and a mountain of paperwork. Most of it, even the grocery ordering lists and letters of recommendation for long-gone parlour maids, they'd decided to keep. It would be the start of a rich family archive, giving glimpses of daily life from the castle over the last fifty years. Faith had suggested having an exhibition, and much to his surprise Marcus had found himself agreeing. In the New Year some time, though, when all this Christmas madness was over.

Faith pulled an old invitation for the Christmas Ball from the nearest pile and lifted it up to show the stuffed badger, who'd been released from his filing cabinet prison and now perched proudly on a wooden plant stand, keeping guard. His beady little orange glass eyes glinted in the light from a single bare bulb overhead.

'What do you think, Basil? Worth keeping?'

Marcus put down the cardboard box full of cups and saucers he'd been moving. 'Basil?'

Faith shrugged. 'Basil the Badger. It seemed to fit.'

Marcus shook his head.

Side by side, they started sorting through piles of assorted papers, books and boxes, stopping every now and then to show each other what they'd found, debating the merits of each find.

It was nice to have someone to discuss things with—even if it was whether to keep a receipt for a peacock feather evening bag or not. It made him realise just how much he'd been on his own since he'd come back to Hadsborough to work. He only discussed the bigger issues with his grandfather, leaving him to rest. The remainder Marcus dealt with by himself.

It had been different in the City. He'd had plenty of friends, an active social life, a woman who'd said she loved him…

Better not to think of her. She was long gone with the rest of them. Everyone he'd counted on had deserted him when he'd needed them most. It seemed the family name had been more of a draw than he'd thought, and once that had been dragged through the mud they'd scattered. Whether it was because he was no longer useful or they thought they'd be painted guilty by association didn't matter.

But now he was back home, with only an elderly relative for company. The staff kept a respectful distance, not only because he was the boss, but because of the family he'd been born into. He realised he hadn't had much time to socialise with people who weren't afraid to meet him as an equal, as a human being instead of a title.

Faith did that. Without being disrespectful or fake. Not many people achieved that balance, and he appreciated it. She wasn't afraid to share her opinions, but she was never argumentative or rude. She just 'called a spade a spade', as his grandmother had used to say. In fact he had some news for her about one of their recent conversations when she'd done just that.

'It's been four days since we cut the ticket prices to the Christmas Ball and sent word around the village,' he said nonchalantly as he dusted off a pile of old seventy-eight records. 'And relaxed the dress code, of course.'

Faith stopped what she was doing and turned round. Her ponytail swung over her shoulder and he got the most intoxicating whiff of camellias and rose petals.

'Yeah? Have sales improved?'

He nodded. 'The locals are snapping them up.'

Her eyebrows rose. 'See? I told you I understood the community spirit you get in a place like this. People just love to feel involved. You're not their lords and masters any more, so it wouldn't hurt to stop hiding away in your castle and mix a little.'

He snorted. 'I do not hide away in my castle.'

She raised her eyebrows. 'Oh, no? When was the last time you went down to the village pub for a drink, then?'

'I could name you a time and a date,' he said, sounding a little smug.

Faith wasn't fooled for a second. 'Sock it to me.'

Marcus closed his eyes and smiled as he looked away for a second. 'Okay, I was seventeen,' he said as he met her impish gaze, 'and I escaped down to the village with a couple of my schoolfriends who were staying over. The village bobby had to bring us back at two in the morning, drunk as skunks. I was grounded for a month. So I remember that occasion very well.'

'It wouldn't hurt you to get outside the boundaries of the estate once in a while, you know.'

He wanted to argue, to say he did—but hadn't he just been thinking about being on his own so much? Had he turned himself into a hermit? Surely not.

'You will come, won't you?' he asked.

'To the village pub? Now, there's an offer a gal can't refuse!' She gave him a wry smile as she took a vinyl record from his hands and inspected it.

'No,' he said, 'to the Christmas Ball.'

She rubbed a bit of dust that he'd missed off the corner of the record sleeve with her fingers. 'It would be lovely, but I…I can't. I'm busy with the window, and a ball's not really my sort of thing.'

'You said you were making good progress,' he replied. He looked around the darkening cellar. The sky through the narrow windows at the top of the room was indigo now. 'An invitation is the least I can give you after all you've done to help resurrect the idea.'

If anything she looked sadder. 'Maybe,' was all she said.

He didn't get it. He thought women liked balls and dressing up and dancing. So why had Faith sounded as if he'd asked her if he could gently roast the family rabbit for dinner? Perhaps he'd better change the subject.

He picked the next record up from the pile. 'What about this Christmas-mad small town you come from? Tell me about your family.'

Faith shrugged and handed him back the first seventy-eight. 'Gram is the only one who lives in Beckett's Run now. One sister lives in Sydney, the other travels all over for work, and my mother just…drifts.'

She wandered off to the other side of the room and started nosing around in a cardboard box over there.

Hmm… One minute she was spouting on about community spirit and getting involved, but the first mention of home and family and she was off like a shot. What was all that about?

He decided it was none of his business. He didn't like people poking around in his family's affairs, and maybe Faith didn't either. Instead of pursuing the matter further he concentrated on the pile of records—a few of which he suspected were collectors' items—and they worked in silence again after that. Not so comfortable this time, however.

He checked his watch again after he'd glanced up to see the sky outside was inky black. Faith saw his movement and stopped what she was doing.

'Time to call it a day,' he said.

She nodded from behind her high stone walls. 'Good. I'm starving.'

He walked over to the plastic crates and put his most recent finds next to the old records in the top one. He snapped the lid back on, then made his way to the door. He tugged the handle, and it turned, but the door itself didn't budge. He tried again. Not even a groan. The heavy oak door was stuck fast. Old Mr Grey had cautioned him to use the doorstop, and up until this evening he had, but Faith had been the last one in and he'd forgotten to share that vital bit of information with her.

And now they were trapped in here. Alone.

CHAPTER SIX

Behind him, Faith groaned. 'Really? Stuck in the castle dungeons?'

'They're not dungeons,' he reminded her calmly. 'No leg irons or racks here. It's just a cellar.'

'Can we open a window? Yell for help?'

He marched over to the first high window and tugged at the metal loop. Also stuck. However, he had better luck with the next one along. The window was hinged at the bottom, and he managed to pull it open so there was a gap of four or five inches at the top. A small shower of crunchy snow landed on his arm and he brushed it away before dragging a smallish wooden table over to stand underneath. Once he was sure it would take his weight he stood on it, so his face was near to the opening and shouted.

They waited.

Nothing.

He tried again.

Same result.

'Here… Maybe two voices are better than one.'

Before he realised what she was doing, Faith jumped up and joined him on the table. She wobbled as her back foot joined the other one and instinctively grabbed on to the front of his jumper for support. Marcus looked down at her. Her eyes were wide and her breath was coming in little gasps. His brain told him it was just the shock of almost tumbling down onto the hard stone floor, but his body told him something rather different.

Kiss her, it said.

Faith's mouth had been slightly open, but she closed it now, even as her eyes grew larger.

Nothing happened. Nobody moved. He wasn't even sure either of them breathed. He could read it in her face. She'd had exactly the same thought at the same time, and she was equally frozen, stuck between doing the sensible thing and doing what her instincts were telling her to do.

He wasn't sure who moved first. Maybe they both did at the same time. Her fingers uncurled from the front of his sweater and she dropped her head. He looked away. It seemed neither of them were ready to take that leap.

He turned back to the window and yelled, venting all his frustration through the narrow gap. After a second Faith joined him. When they were out of breath they waited, side by side and silent, for anything—the sound of footsteps, another voice. All they heard was the lap of water against the edge of the path outside and the distant squawk of a goose.

He jumped down from the table, got some distance between them. 'There's nobody out there. Too cold, too dark.'

Faith sat down on the table and then slid onto the floor. She stayed close to it, gripping on to the edge with one hand and tracing the fingers of the other over its grainy surface. 'What about people inside the castle?'

He shook his head. 'The walls are at least a foot thick. I doubt if the sound even left this room.' He checked his watch. 'It's not long until dinner, though. Someone will miss us soon.'

She nodded, but still looked concerned.

Marcus knew she had good reason to. Another hour, at least, and he'd already thought about kissing her once. Thankfully he had a solution to their current predicament that his ancestors wouldn't have had. He pulled his mobile phone from his pocket.

Signals in the area could be patchy, especially near the castle. He checked the display on his phone. One minuscule bar of signal, but maybe that was enough. He tried dialling the estate office, just in case anyone was still there. His phone beeped at him. *Call failed.* The signal indicator on his phone was now a cross instead of any bars. Damn.

'No signal,' he said to Faith. It seemed these thick stone walls could withstand any means of escape.

She jumped up onto the table again. 'Here. Pass it to me.'

Silently he handed his phone over, and she held it up to the window and pressed a button to redial. He held his breath, but a few moments later she shook her head and handed the phone back to him.

'Try sending a text. I've worked in plenty of old buildings, including basements, and sometimes I can get texts even if I can't receive calls.'

He nodded and tapped in a message to Shirley. She always kept her phone in her pocket. In a home like his, sometimes shouting up the stairs wasn't enough. Mobiles were usually pretty reliable—but obviously not when most of the room was underground and surrounded by water.

An icon appeared, telling him it was sending, but a minute later his phone was still chugging away. The blasted thing wouldn't go.

He put the handset up near the window, balancing it on the frame. 'Better chance of getting a signal,' he said. 'Now we just need to wait.'

He stole a look at her. Her mask of composure was back in place. No one would guess that moments ago she'd been flushed and breathless, lips slightly parted... It was as if that moment on top of the table had never happened.

Right there. That was why his warning bells rang—why he shouldn't think about kissing her. It had nothing to do with her nationality or her background, and everything to do with Faith herself.

The woman who lived behind those high walls of hers—Technicolor Faith—would be very easy to fall for. He felt he'd always known her, had been waiting for her to stroll across his lawn and come crashing into his life. He could feel that familiar tug, that naïve, misguided urge to lay everything he had and everything he was at her feet.

But that ability of hers to disconnect, to detach herself emotionally, was what kept him backing off. At least Amanda had tried; Faith McKinnon would always be just a fingertip out of reach.

Coward.

He ignored the voice inside his head, knowing he was right. He wasn't going to be that weak ever again. So he decided he needed to do something to fill the rest of the time rather than just stand close to her, staring at her.

Conversation would be good. It would stop him thinking about doing other things with his lips. But Faith had already resisted his attempt to talk about her family, so he needed another subject. Thankfully, he knew her favourite one. If he could get her talking about the window the hour would fly by.

'You believe Samuel Crowbridge made the window, don't you?' he asked.

She trapped her bottom lip under her teeth and then let it slide slowly out again, exhaling hard, as if she didn't quite want to say what she was about to say. Marcus tried not to watch, tried not to imagine what it would feel like if it were not her teeth but his lips…

'Yes…yes. I do,' she said, and that light he'd been both dreading and waiting for crept into her eyes. 'But believing isn't enough. I need solid proof.'

'For yourself? Or for others?'

She looked perplexed. 'Both. You can't put stock in dreams

and wishes, can you? At some point you have to have hard evidence.'

Marcus frowned. 'Sometimes one doesn't have that luxury,' he said, his tone bare. 'Sometimes you just have to do without.'

That was what he'd done after his father's death. No one had really known the truth of what had happened. He'd tried very hard to believe what people had said—that it had just been an accident—but the collapse of the family firm had started him questioning everything about his father, and he hadn't been able to shake the cynical little voice inside his head.

'Of course hard evidence is preferable, but it's not always there. Sometimes you just have to take a leap and hope you're jumping in the right direction,' he added.

Faith gave him a weary look. 'Unfortunately the academic community don't share your faith in gut instincts.'

'Have you found anything more about the other painting? Hope, wasn't it?'

She shook her head. 'Not much. The family who own it aren't ones for sharing. I can't even find a picture of it. They also own any sketches and documents pertaining to the original commission, so it's unlikely I'll get any confirmation from that source.' She opened the rolltop of an old bureau that had previously been blocked by a hatstand, and coughed as the dust flew into the air. 'That's why finding something here at Hadsborough is so important. It could be my only chance.'

As she searched a small smile curved her lips. He instinctively knew she was thinking about something that amused her.

'What?'

She rolled her eyes. 'A goofy coincidence. It's just that the names of the three paintings are almost a match for me and my two sisters.'

Marcus's eyebrows lifted. 'Faith, Hope and Charity?'

She walked towards him slowly. 'No, my littlest sister would have gone nuts if that was the case. Mom switched Charity to Grace.'

'What are the odds?' he muttered. 'Are you the oldest?'

She shook her head and leaned against the desk next to him. 'Mom never was one for sticking to convention. I'm in the middle. We all used to complain about our names, of course. Can you imagine the teasing we got at school?'

He made a wry face. 'I went to an all-boys boarding school. If that's not an education in just how abominable children can be, I don't know what is.'

She nodded in sympathy. 'Grace complains the most, even though I think she's got the best end of the deal.' She gave him a devilish little grin. 'But when we were younger Hope and I had a way of shutting her up.'

'Oh, yes?'

She nodded, then smiled to herself at the memory. 'We used to tease her that Gram had talked Mom out of calling her Chastity, so she could have had it a whole lot worse!'

He couldn't help laughing, and she grinned back at him before hopping up and sitting at the other end of the table. They weren't touching. *Quite.*

She'd forgotten to put those barriers back down, hadn't she? Even though they'd veered off the subject of the window and onto something more personal. He should say something to kill this moment, move away…

But he didn't. Just a few more seconds to find out what really lay beneath Faith's high walls. The chance might not come again, and he'd be safe once she retreated behind them once more. She always did.

'It sounds as if you're close,' he said.

Faith's smile disappeared. 'Not really. Not any more. It all changed after…'

He shifted so his body faced hers more fully. 'After what?'

'You don't want to know. It's too…' She shook her head and closed her eyes. 'Your family…they're so different to mine.'

He guessed she was talking about somebody having misbehaved. 'You'd be surprised what the rich and powerful get up to just because they can,' he said, a dry tone to his voice. 'The second Duke was a bigamist, the third Duke had more illegitimate children than he could count and the fourth Duke lost Hadsborough in a drunken game of dice and won it back again the next night. And those are just the highlights. There are plenty more stories to tell about the Huntingtons.'

Faith shook her head, but she was smiling. 'Not the same, and you know it. All those things make your family sound dashing and exciting. My family just makes people shake their heads and look sad.'

A stab of something hit Marcus square in the chest. Suddenly Faith wasn't the only one on the edge of revealing something big.

'Oh, mine make people shake their heads and look sad, too,' he said.

'No, they don't…' Faith began, laughing gently, assuming he was teasing. But when she met his eyes the laughter died. 'They do?' she said, blinking in disbelief.

They did. And he found that for the first time in over eighteen months he wanted to tell someone about it. Someone who wasn't connected. Someone who *didn't care,* who wouldn't invest. He suddenly realised that Faith's walls made her the perfect candidate.

'I worked for my father until just before he died,' he said, his voice deceptively flat and unemotional. 'He'd started up an investment company thirty years before, and things were going really well… At least I thought they were.' He shook his head. 'I should have seen it coming. He was always so sure of himself—too sure—as if he thought he was indestructible. It made for great business when the markets were good. He liked to take risks, you see, and they often paid off.'

She nodded, waited for him to continue.

'But in the last few years, with the way the financial climate had been—' he made a face '—being *daring* didn't cut it any more. In fact he lost a lot of people a lot of money. But my father was gripped by the unswerving belief that he could turn it around. He kept risking, kept gambling, kept losing… The company went bust. People lost their jobs.' He looked her straight in the eye. 'I knew what he was like, even though I didn't know the extent of his recklessness. I should have done more. I should have stopped him.'

'It wasn't your fault, Marcus, what your father did. He made his own choices.'

Marcus swallowed. That was what he'd been afraid of.

Not on the business front. People had called Harvey Huntington a swindler, but that hadn't been true. He'd just had an unshakeable belief in himself, hadn't thought he could fail so badly. And when he had… Well, the unshakeable man had been shaken to the core. He'd never quite recovered.

'About a year later they found his car wrapped round a lamp post,' he added baldly.

Faith gasped and her hand covered her mouth. 'I'm so sorry,' she said. 'I didn't know.'

'The inquest ruled it an accident,' he said, nodding to himself. 'He'd been drinking, and he never did like to wear his seat belt. But there were rumours…'

Faith's eyes grew wide. 'You mean that he'd *meant* to do it?'

Marcus just looked at her. 'That's about the gist of it.'

'You don't believe that, do you?' she said, horrified.

'I try not to.'

Faith reached over and laid her hand on his arm. He looked down at it. They hadn't touched since their first meeting, and that one simple, spontaneous gesture completely arrested him. He looked back at her face—really looked at her—and saw warmth and compassion and gentle strength. Instead of climbing back behind her walls, he could feel she was reaching out to him, and it made him ache for her in an entirely new way.

No. He couldn't want this. Shouldn't.

But he could feel himself slipping, forgetting why.

'You can't take the blame for this, Marcus. It was nothing to do with you.' She shook her head as she talked. 'You can't carry this round with you, believe me. For your own sanity you have to find a way to separate yourself, to disconnect.'

That pulled him up short. She was good at that, wasn't she? He needed to remember that.

'Is that what you did?'

She stopped shaking her head. 'I beg your pardon?'

'Disconnect?' he said. 'I might be too wrapped up in my family, but you seem cast adrift from yours. Is that how you cope? Running away? Living in a different country? I can't do that, Faith. I have to stay and fight—for Bertie, for my children and their children.'

He knew he sounded angry, but he couldn't seem to stop himself. He was angry with her for showing him parts of herself she'd never let him have, at his father for leaving him in such a mess, even at Hadsborough for the way it hung around his neck like a millstone. Telling her the truth had opened a floodgate. And he needed desperately to break this sense of intimacy weaving its way around them both and binding them together. He needed to push her away, to make that soft compassion completely disappear from her eyes.

She pulled her hand back and glared at him, and he knew his accusations had struck home. He should have been pleased.

'You don't know anything about me, so don't you dare judge.'

'I'm not judging you,' he said. 'You're right. I don't know anything about you. Because every time anyone asks you block them out.' It irritated him that she'd been able to run from her family, to taste freedom, when he'd been trapped by his. 'So shock me. Tell me. Tell me what awful thing happened to make you avoid your home and family like the plague.'

Faith looked up at him, her eyes huge, and swallowed. For a few hot seconds she'd been furious, but then something else had crept up on her and taken her completely by surprise—the urge to do just what he suggested.

Could she tell him? Would it really be as easy as that? She never wanted to talk about this. Not to anyone. And especially not to the rest of her family.

But he wasn't family. And she was thousands of miles away in a soundproof cellar. Somehow it seemed safer to let the words out here than anywhere else.

Also, Marcus had shared something incredibly painful and personal with her, and she couldn't ignore the sense of imbalance that left her with. She needed to get them back on an equal footing again so she could put her defences in place.

'You…' she said, shaking her head. 'You've always known who you are, where you belong in the world. I don't know if I can explain it…' She swallowed. It had been so long since she'd talked about this with anyone that she didn't know if the words were still there. 'I don't know where to start,' she whispered.

He held her gaze. There was still fire in his eyes, but it was softening, brightening. 'Try the beginning,' he said in a low voice.

Faith nodded and moistened her lips. 'My mom… She's a bit of a…'

How did she put this? Calling your own mother a flake out loud, no matter how many times you did it in your head, did not seem right.

She shrugged. 'She likes to move around, has sudden passions for hobbies or places—even people—that are all-consuming.' Faith looked down at her denim-clad thighs. 'While they last. And they never do last.'

Marcus gave her his half-smile, the one that curved the right side of his mouth so deliciously. 'A bit like Bertie, then?'

She gave an exasperated puff. 'No way! Bertie is sweet and charming. Mom… Well, Mom is just…infuriating.'

He laughed a dry little huff of a laugh. 'And you don't think I find my grandfather the slightest bit exasperating?'

Faith pinned her bottom lip in the centre with her top teeth. Okay, maybe he had a point there. But she doubted he'd find her mother sweet and charming. Nutty as a squirrel, maybe.

'The same pattern applied to her marriage. She and my dad were on again, off again, for so long. And then one day he'd had enough of trying to make her see sense and he left. Or that's what I thought at the time.'

Marcus nodded. 'My mother left my father under very similar circumstances. She loved him, even though he was a bit of a cad, but she couldn't deal with all that and this place as well. Eventually she had enough.'

A well of sympathy opened up inside Faith. She knew just what that was like, to see a parent leave, promising it was nothing to do with you, that it was the grown-ups who were to blame.

'How old were you?' she whispered.

'Nine,' he replied baldly.

She nodded. Almost the same age she had been when Greg McKinnon had left the family home for the final time. She reckoned she and Marcus had more in common than she'd first thought.

'You stayed here?' she asked.

'I was at boarding school most of the time. And holidays were shared between both parents. I felt slightly divorced from the whole thing, to be honest, as if it wasn't really happening—until I came home for my summer holiday when I was thirteen and there was a new, young, blonde Lady

Westerham installed in my father's suite, wanting me to call her Mummy, and the reality of the whole situation suddenly became very clear.'

'Ouch,' she said.

Marcus smiled grimly. 'You have a gift for coming up with exactly the right word for the occasion, do you know that?'

Faith smiled softly back. 'Gram says I may not say a lot, but what I do say packs a punch.'

'Smart lady,' he said, his mouth stretching into a proper smile this time.

Faith's heart began to hammer.

She sighed. 'That wasn't all, though. But it seems so lame compared to what you've just told me.' She got up, fetched her wallet from her purse and pulled out a crinkled photograph of three women. She pointed to the polished blonde on the right. 'That's Hope,' she said, and then she tapped a blunt fingernail against the girl on the left, her fair hair caught in ponytail. 'And that's Grace.'

And there in the middle was Faith. Shorter, darker, not as pretty.

'I can see the family resemblance,' he said quietly.

Faith decided not to swallow her next comment, not to let it echo round her head as she usually did. Instead she said it out loud. 'Between the two of *them*.' She pulled in some dusty air and tucked the wallet into her jeans pocket.

The tiniest lift of Marcus's eyebrows was his only response.

'The reason my dad left was because he found out he wasn't really my dad at all. Mom had an affair years earlier, during one of their frequent bust-ups. She never told him, and when he found out it was the final straw.'

Marcus didn't say anything, but the fierce compassion in his eyes was enough to make her throat clog. When she'd first met Marcus she'd thought he was uptight and superior, but it wasn't that at all. He wasn't mean; he just was fiercely protective of those he cared about. And, dammit, if that didn't make him more appealing. She'd always been a sucker for loyalty.

The penny dropped, and she suddenly understood why those glowering looks of his got to her so. She'd always yearned for someone to look out for her that way, instead of feeling she was on her own, always having to look out for herself. One of her fathers had vanished before she'd even been born, and the other had left before she'd become a teenager. She couldn't imagine Marcus vanishing on anybody. Oh, how she could have used a man like him in her life when she was younger.

She looked at her feet, dangling off the edge of the table. 'They didn't tell me until I was eighteen, but I'd always suspected something was wrong.'

'He carried on being a father to you after he left the family home?'

She nodded. 'He's a good man, but very practical and structured—not really a good match for my mom. All three of us girls used to go and stay with him at weekends, but I could tell even then. There was something about the way he looked at me—'

She broke off, unable to continue for a moment.

'There was always this…pain in his eyes.' A giant breath deflated her ribcage. 'He didn't look at the other girls that way,' she added as she looked up at him and tried to smile. 'It was a relief to find out in some ways.'

Moisture fell hot and fast from her lashes. This was stupid. She never cried. And how selfish to cry for herself, when she really should be crying for him and all he'd had to face.

She sniffed and dragged the back of her hand across one cheek and then the other. 'I finally understood why I'd always felt the odd one out, but it didn't stop me feeling that way. If anything I felt even more of a fraud.' She shook her head and looked up at him. 'I'm glad you've still got your grandfather after all that's happened to you, to give you that sense of balance and belonging. It's a horrible thing to not know who you are and where you fit in.'

He reached for her hand. She saw his brain working behind his eyes, and his gaze sharpened and became more penetrating as his fingers covered hers. 'You said the first time we met that your father was English?'

She nodded. 'He ran a bookshop in Beckett's Run for a few years. I don't even remember what he looks like, apart from the fact he has dark hair like mine and that he always smiled at me when we visited the store. He gave me a book once. Fairytales, with a picture of Rapunzel on the cover. Inside it was full of castles, princesses and noble knights.' She paused and gave a self-conscious shrug. 'Kind of like this one.'

Marcus's eyes warmed. 'Castle, yes. The princesses and noble knights are long gone.'

Faith lowered her lids for a moment. She wasn't so sure about the noble knights. She reckoned there was one sitting right next to her, his strong hand over hers as he patiently listened to her whine on about her family. Most men she knew would run a mile at the sight of female tears.

'It was my favourite book,' she whispered softly, 'even before I knew who he was.'

'He must be very proud of you,' Marcus said, and another unexpected stab of pain got her in the gut.

'He doesn't know me.'

Marcus looked shocked. 'He's never tried to find you? Or you him?'

She shook her head. 'I'm not sure he even knows about me. And it was almost thirty years ago… He's probably got a wife and other kids now. He doesn't need me blasting in from the past and upturning everything.'

And she didn't need to invade a family she had no place in. She'd tried that once—tried so hard—and it had all fallen apart around her. She wasn't going to make that mistake again.

'He's your father. Of course he'll want to see you. How could he not?'

The look in his eyes—as if he totally believed what he was saying, that it wouldn't be just one more round of rejection—made something tiny and wavering flicker to life inside her.

And he saw it. Right deep inside her, he saw it.

Marcus was looking down at her, his jaw set, but there was a new and disarming softness in those clear blue eyes. Faith's pulse began to thunder inside her veins. Everything was still. Even the ever-vocal geese outside were quiet.

Slowly Marcus lifted his hand to her face, brushed the tips of his fingers along her cheekbone. Her eyes slid closed and she breathed in a delicious little shiver as her head tipped back.

She knew what was coming. Had known it was coming ever since that first meeting more than a week ago, when she'd slid her hand into his on that misty morning. She just hadn't realised how much she'd been waiting for it, or how badly she'd wanted it.

His lips touched hers, so gently, so softly, it made her want to cry all over again. She'd expected fierceness, but if anything this tenderness was more devastating. She met him, moved her lips against his, but she didn't want to rush, didn't want to hurry. This was too sweet, too perfect. She wanted to suspend this moment in time and make it last for ever.

His breath was warm against her mouth, and she couldn't resist touching her tongue softly to his bottom lip, tasting him, drawing in that warmth. He shuddered in response, and something swelled within her even as she sensed him resist the urge to use his superior strength to pull her to him and lose himself in her.

Faith had never wanted to be thought of as fragile. She was tough. She could cope. She could batten down the hatches and make it through. But the way he held her, touched her, as if she was made of delicate glass, unravelled something inside her—something she hadn't even been aware had been wound up tight.

He paused for a moment, pulled his lips gently from hers with exquisite softness. Just as he was about to kiss her again, just as sensitive skin was about to meet sensitive skin, there was an almighty crash on the other side of the room.

He jumped up, and Faith was left there sitting on the table, eyes closed, mouth more than ready. At first she thought one of the haphazard piles of stuff had finally given in to gravity, but when she opened her eyes and followed Marcus's trail through the dust she realised what was going on.

It was the door. Someone was trying to ram it open from the other side. They were saved.

Faith slid off the table, hugged her arms around herself and watched. Marcus yelled instructions from their side, and more crashes against the sturdy old wooden door followed. She could see it moving, millimetre by millimetre.

Using the table to gain extra height, she retrieved Marcus's phone from the window frame. The text had sent itself more than fifteen minutes ago.

Marcus stood back from the door as one final shove from the other side unjammed the slab of oak and a burly man stumbled into the room under the force of his own momentum. Marcus moved forward to check he was all right.

Faith didn't move.

She couldn't. A whole squadron of butterflies were doing aerial acrobatics in her stomach. She couldn't do anything but watch Marcus, wait for his gaze to connect with hers again, to see if the look in his eyes confirmed that what had just happened between them had really happened, that it hadn't all just been a dream.

Marcus thanked the man, shook his hand then picked the doorstop up with a flourish and wedged it under the open door. Only when that was done did he lift his head and look at her. The butterflies started dive-bombing.

It was real. It had been real.

Oh, jeepers. What was she going to do now?

Suddenly her feet were free and she found herself jogging towards the door. She grinned at the burly man, thanking him profusely, knowing she was overdoing it and sounding like a clown in a sideshow. She moved to pass him, to cross the threshold and escape.

'Faith...' A hand shot out and caught her wrist, but so lightly that she could pull away if she wanted to.

She wanted to.

Marcus's words were left hanging in the air. She licked her lips and looked away, trying not to think about the feel of his mouth there, the soft promises he'd silently delivered. Promises that shouldn't exist. Promises he couldn't keep. She looked away.

'I'll see you at dinner,' she muttered, sliding her wrist from his grasp. Then she placed his phone into his empty hand and ran up the spiral stone staircase to the ground floor.

CHAPTER SEVEN

DINNER was quiet. Faith had spent a lot of it looking in his direction without actually looking *at* him. She didn't avoid his gaze entirely, but when she did meet his eyes her expression was blank, empty. Disconnected.

Marcus felt a tug of guilt deep down in his gut, even though in the moments before their lips had touched she'd tipped her head back and all but invited him to kiss her. He hadn't meant to make her feel like this.

When instead of joining him and his grandfather in the drawing room after dinner she excused herself and headed upstairs, Marcus followed. His grandfather's eyes glittered as he left the room. Sly old fox.

Marcus caught up with her on the wide stone staircase. 'Faith!' he called softly.

She stopped, but didn't turn.

He closed the gap.

She started to move again, but he reached for her, hooking the ends of his curled fingers into hers, and that was all it took to stop her. She stared into the distance, even though the thick wall was only ten feet in front of her.

He gently moved the tips of his fingers, feeling the smaller, sensitive pads of hers beneath his own. Her head snapped round and she looked at him.

He saw it all, then—the tug of war happening behind her eyes. Something in her expression melted, met him.

'We need to talk,' he said.

She didn't nod, didn't say anything, but he saw the agreement in her eyes. However, now he had her where he wanted her he wasn't sure what to say. *Sorry?* He realised he didn't want to—because he wasn't. Those few stolen moments in the cellar had tasted like freedom.

He took a leap, giving her more honesty than he'd planned to. 'I've wanted to do that since almost the first moment I met you,' he said.

Faith let out a heavy breath, her eyes still locked on his. Once again he felt that sense of accord, harmony—and a hint of wry acknowledgement.

She shook her head and looked at their linked fingers before returning her gaze to his face. 'You? Me? I don't know what this is…' She pressed her free hand to her breastbone. 'But it can't go anywhere, even if we want it to.'

God, he wanted it to. The force of that realisation hit him like a thunderclap. It didn't help that he knew she was right. Neither of them wanted this, were ready for this.

He let go of her hand. Her eyes shimmered with regret, and a little sadness. He breathed out hard.

'It's only a couple of weeks,' she said, 'and then I'll be gone. Can we try to keep it professional until then—or at the very least platonic?'

He heard the hidden plea, knew she was balancing on a knife-edge, just as he was, torn between doing what was right and what felt right. Suddenly he had the overwhelming urge to protect her, save her. It washed over him in a warm wave, starting at his toes and ending at his ears, and then settled into a small hard rock inside his chest.

He nodded. 'Goodnight, Faith,' he said, his voice low.

Her eyes filled with silent gratitude. 'Goodnight, Marcus.'

It was only as he watched her walk up the stairs that he realised he was protecting her from himself.

Faith did her best to keep busy the next day. She got to the studio early, determined to remove the last of the glass from the old lead. Each fragment she removed was placed on the carefully drawn template she'd made. It was slow work, but absorbing, and it kept her mind off things she didn't want to think about. However, as the hand on the clock moved closer to four her heart-rate refused to settle into its normal rhythm.

Would he come?

At four-fifteen she had her answer. There was a rap on the door, but this time, instead of opening it a split-second later, he waited for her reply. Marcus was good with boundaries, she realised. He wouldn't overstep their agreement, and she knew she wouldn't have to remind him of it even once in the coming fortnight. So why didn't that make her feel any happier?

'Come in,' she called, feeling her own boundaries crumble a little further, like the scattering of grit and pebbles just before a rock-fall. Mentally, she shored them up as best she could.

'Hello,' he said.

His expression was shuttered, wary. It was almost the way he'd looked at her on that first morning, except... She had the oddest feeling that although the walls were back it wasn't that he was pushing her away, but holding himself back.

She cleared her throat. 'Hi.'

Platonic, she'd said. And Marcus had wanted to be informed of any interesting developments regarding the window. She could do this. She could do platonic and professional. She'd never had any problems with it before.

'Come and see.' She indicated the half pulled apart window on the table in front of her.

He nodded and, just as he'd done for the whole of the previous week, asked thoughtful, intelligent questions. She

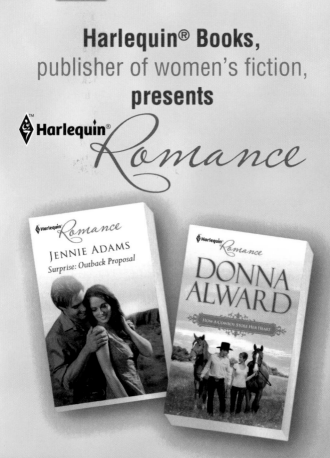

GET 2 BOOKS

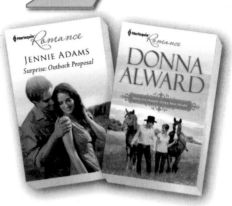

We'd like to send you two *Harlequin® Romance*
novels absolutely free. Accepting them puts you under
no obligation to purchase any more books.

HOW TO GET YOUR
2 FREE BOOKS AND 2 FREE GIFTS

1. Return the reply card today, and we'll send you two
   Harlequin Romance novels, absolutely free! We'll even
   pay the postage!

2. Accepting free books places you under no obligation
   to buy anything, ever. Whatever you decide, the free
   books and gifts are yours to keep, free!

3. We hope that after receiving your free books you'll
   want to remain a subscriber, but the choice is yours—
   to continue or cancel, any time at all!

EXTRA BONUS

**You'll also get two free mystery gifts!
(worth about $10)**

FREE!

▶ DETACH AND MAIL CARD TODAY! ▶

Return this card today to get
2 FREE BOOKS and 2 FREE GIFTS!

Harlequin® *Romance*

YES! Please send me 2 FREE *Harlequin® Romance* novels,
and 2 FREE mystery gifts as well. I understand I am
under no obligation to purchase anything,
as explained on the back of this insert.

❏ I prefer the regular-print edition
116/316 HDL FMPU

❏ I prefer the larger-print edition
186/386 HDL FMPU

Please Print

FIRST NAME   LAST NAME

ADDRESS

APT.#   CITY

STATE/PROV.   ZIP/POSTAL CODE

Visit us at:
www.ReaderService.com

H-R-04/12

If offer card is missing, write to: The Reader Service, P.O. Box 1867, Buffalo, NY 14240-1867 or visit www.ReaderService.com

BUSINESS REPLY MAIL
FIRST-CLASS MAIL   PERMIT NO. 717   BUFFALO, NY

POSTAGE WILL BE PAID BY ADDRESSEE

THE READER SERVICE
PO BOX 1867
BUFFALO NY 14240-9952

NO POSTAGE
NECESSARY
IF MAILED
IN THE
UNITED STATES

answered him clearly, adding in interesting facts, which had also become her habit. Anyone watching them would have thought nothing had changed, that what had happened in the cellar had stayed in the cellar.

Faith knew better.

The whole time they talked there was an undercurrent that hadn't been there before, pulsing away beneath the surface.

And they didn't deny it—to themselves or each other— but by tacit agreement decided to leave it be. It was frustrating, but it was honest. She didn't think she could have lied to him anyway. Somehow he could see inside her. It wasn't that she'd let her barriers fall—they were still tightly in place— but that to him, and only him, they were like the glass on the table in front of her.

'I've asked Shirley to rustle up some help with the cellar,' he said. 'She's sending a couple of the part-time cleaning staff down. There should be waiting for us by the time we get there.'

She nodded, knowing this was a good idea—a fabulous idea—even as her heart sank. It was a good idea to give Basil some back-up.

'Hope they like dust,' she said as she grabbed her coat, 'and badgers...'

Marcus's father had always accused him of being a contrary child with an iron will, and now that resolve served him well. Even so, the cellar-cleaning crew became his safety net over the next few days, stopping him giving in to the urge to 'lose' the doorstop one evening and do something stupid.

It didn't help him forget, though. He couldn't erase the memory of that kiss, that sweet, soft, *unfinished* kiss.

From the way Faith's gaze would snag with his, the way she'd colour and look away, he guessed she was suffering the same way. But she'd asked for friendship alone. They had an agreement and he was honouring it.

They were both back safely behind their respective walls of polite friendliness. That should have been enough, but it wasn't helping. Walls that were three feet thick were a great idea, but if those walls were transparent…

It made the whole thing worse. Now he could see Technicolor Faith all the time, but he knew he couldn't—shouldn't—reach out and touch her. Even so, he could feel his resolve slipping a little more every day. It had started with his wanting to keep her safe, to protect her, and now he was starting to want to give her other things. Things he hadn't realised he still had left to give. Maybe he didn't. And they were things Faith McKinnon didn't even want.

He just had to keep it all together for another ten days. That was all.

Late Friday morning he was passing the studio and decided to stick his head in. He found her not hunched over the table, as usual, but sitting back on her stool, hands on hips, staring at the last remaining pieces of dirty glass that she had been cleaning.

'Problem?' he said as he came and stood behind her, trying to see what was so perplexing.

She shook her head. 'Not a problem…just some interesting irregularities.'

'Not anything to do with a message?' He shaved the words *I hope* off the end of that sentence.

'No.'

He pulled up another stool and sat down next to her. 'Talk me through it.' This was safe enough territory.

She pushed her stool back, stood up and walked over to a second table, where she plucked a large photo of the window from a pile of papers and brought it back to show him. Marcus did his best to concentrate on what was in front of his eyes instead of the faint smell of rose gardens that always seemed to cling to her. What was it? Perfume? Shampoo? Whatever it was, he was finding it very distracting, even though he'd never really had a fondness for the blasted flowers.

She pointed to the top of the photograph. 'See the lead there? It's very fine and it was beautifully crafted. The work of a master glazier. No doubt about it.'

His gaze followed her slender finger down to the bottom of the picture.

'But here…nowhere near the skill. It's as if it's been repaired by a local craftsman just trying to do his best.'

Marcus's eyebrows drew together. 'Maybe the workman wasn't up to the job.'

She nodded. 'Probably. But it's not the fact that the window was repaired, but where and how that's interesting. A breakage results in a certain pattern—either a crack in just one piece of glass, or a wider area of damage radiating out from the point of impact. See this bit down here…?' She pointed to a long, wide section at the bottom of the pane. 'It's just the glass inside that border that's been replaced. All of it. You can see it quite clearly now it's been cleaned.'

She got up and looked at the disassembled window laid out on the end of the table. 'The new glass is of much poorer quality.'

Faith carefully lifted two small pieces of dark green glass and held them up to the light. One was a beautiful clear emerald, the other was slightly muddier in colour, and the newer glass had a large ripple down the centre. She returned the fragments to the template. 'It's as if someone replaced that whole section—a long, thin rectangular section. Not the sort of shape that would come from usual damage.'

'And that's significant?'

She frowned and gave him a serious look, one that made him think he wasn't going to like what she was about to say.

'I can't quite get it out of my head that someone has removed something from the window.'

He pulled in air through his teeth. 'Something like a message?'

For a second she said nothing, but then she pushed out a breath, stood up and ran a hand through her hair. She smiled at him, a weary little twist of her lips. 'Ignore me. I think I'm starting to let the magic and the mystery of this place seep into me.'

He stared at the window. Now she'd mentioned it he could see the long, thin rectangle, could imagine a phrase or word being in the place where there was now plain green glass.

'I don't think we should tell my grandfather about this. Not yet.'

If ever.

She nodded her agreement. 'There's nothing to tell, anyway. Even if there had been something else in the window, we have no way of knowing what it was.'

That was that. He should feel relieved.

He tilted his head, trying to make it look very much as if he concurred, but he couldn't quite get rid of the niggling worry that Faith had stumbled onto something.

Marcus was having an in-depth discussion with Oliver, his events manager, about preparations for the Christmas Ball when Faith came skidding into the long gallery. Her face was aglow and her eyes were shining. He knew she had something to tell him about the window. Even so, he couldn't help but smile.

She grinned back.

Oliver coughed. 'About the florist, My Lord?'

Marcus kept looking at Faith. He waved a hand in the other man's direction. 'I'm sure you're more than capable of dealing with her,' he said. He only half noticed the man's raised eyebrows as he looked between Faith and himself.

'Don't say I didn't warn you,' Oliver's low voice muttered

beside him, but Marcus was focused on the laughter behind Faith's eyes.

'What?' he said, walking towards her.

Her smile flashed wide, reminding him of how the night sky brightened after a firework exploded.

'I found it!'

For a moment his stomach dropped.

'The proof I need,' she added, her expression dimming slightly in reaction to his *non*-reaction.

Proof?

It was as if she'd heard the question that had fired off inside his head. She stepped forward, her hand held up in a calming gesture. 'Samuel Crowbridge proof,' she explained.

He paused for a moment. While he was truly relieved her news had nothing to do with his grandfather's wild goose chase, he realised he was a little disappointed, too.

'How?' he said.

She glanced over her shoulder, looked at the door that led to the main hall—the route out of the castle and back to the studio. 'Have you got a minute?'

Marcus turned round to take his leave from Oliver and discovered the man had disappeared. Oh, well.

Faith looked about her as she headed for the door. 'It's looking awesome in here,' she said.

'I'm glad you like it,' he replied.

And looking lovely it was. Christmas at Hadsborough had always been special when he was younger, but in recent years it had become a chore. Looking at it now, through Faith's eyes, he realised she was right. There was a fourteen-foot Christmas tree in the hall. Crimson candles in all shapes and sizes were dotted around—some in wrought-iron stands, some in hurricane lamps—and greenery was everywhere: holly and ivy and fir branches, draped over mantelpieces, over the door frames, wound round the banister of the staircase and dripping from the minstrels' gallery over the banqueting hall.

There was a noise in the hallway and a few moments later a walking display of red flowers entered the room. Underneath the foliage was a very human pair of legs: sturdy calves finished off with even sturdier shoes. Marcus recognised those shoes. And *now* he caught on to what Oliver had been trying to warn him about.

Janet Dixon. Florist and one-woman tornado.

Her severe salt-and-pepper hairdo appeared from behind the display and she looked around the room approvingly, as if she deemed it good enough for her arrangement.

Faith walked over and touched the papery petal of one of the fire-red poinsettia. 'My grandmother loves these,' she said thoughtfully.

'Just right for the festive season, they are,' Janet replied. 'Bringing wishes for mirth and celebration.'

Faith smiled. 'I'll tell Gram. She'll like that.'

'Oliver is around somewhere if you need assistance,' Marcus said, then cupped Faith's elbow in his hand and steered her from the room. 'Quick!' he whispered in her ear. 'She does all the flowers for the castle, and she'll tell you about every petal in great detail if you stand still long enough.'

Faith chuckled softly and began to jog towards the exit. Marcus kept pace, grinning.

When they reached the oval lawn in front of the castle they slowed to a walk. The day was crisp and sunny and he breathed in the country air. It smelled like December. Like Christmas. And there was the perfect amount of snow for the ball that night—enough to cover the grassy areas and make the castle look magical, but the paths were clear and the roads gritted.

Quite suddenly he stopped and turned to Faith. 'Come tonight,' he said. 'It's going to be a wonderful evening. You'll be sorry if you miss it.'

I'll be sorry if you miss it.

Her nose wrinkled and she grimaced. 'I don't have anything to wear.'

He had an answer for that. One she'd supplied. 'We relaxed the dress code for those that want to, remember? On very good advice.'

She made a soft scoffing noise. 'There's relaxing and then there's *relaxing*. I'm not sure you lowered it enough for jeans and a T-shirt with a few sequins, and that's the best I can do.'

He started walking again. 'Well, if that's the only problem I'm sure we can sort something out.' There were wardrobes full of ballgowns in the castle. Surely one would fit Faith? He glanced her way. 'That *is* the only problem, isn't it?'

Faith said nothing, just kept walking towards the studio, eyes straight ahead. She was glad Marcus couldn't see her face, if only for a few moments. She needed time to let the emotion show, let those stupid feelings free, before clamping everything down again.

She'd been so elated when she'd run into the castle to tell him of her discovery, but now all that was squelched beneath the slow and persistent ache in her chest. She couldn't go to a ball. Who did she think she was? Cinderella? Real life didn't work out that way. That was why they called them fairy *stories*. And she was doing her best to remember that, she really was.

You don't belong here, she told herself. *You will never belong here. Don't set yourself up for more pain by buying into the dream.*

She opened the studio door when she reached it and walked inside, back to her work table. Something solid here, at least. This wasn't clinging on to fantasies and false hope. She had proof.

She picked up the piece of glass that made up the kneeling woman's lower leg and bare foot, walked over to the large picture window and held it up. She knew the moment Marcus joined her because the air beside her warmed up.

Holding the fragment carefully between thumb and finger at the edges, she pointed to the edge with a finger from the other hand. 'I found this while I was cleaning the glass—getting rid of the dirt and grime and removing the old grout.'

Marcus leaned closer, inspecting the glass, and Faith braced her free hand on the window, hoping it would stop her quivering. So much for everything staying platonic. Somehow the *look but don't touch* agreement she'd manoeuvred him into had intensified everything, done the opposite of what she'd hoped.

'There's writing,' he said, 'scratched into the glass.'

She nodded. 'It's not unusual to find names and dates on fragments of window—little messages from the craftsmen who made or repaired it. Sometimes they are high up in cathedral windows, where nobody would ever see them, just the maker's secret message that no one knows to look for.'

He looked at her. 'So you *did* find a message in the window?'

'Yes, I did. Just not the one we were looking for.'

We? Not *we. You.* It wasn't her quest. She needed to remember that.

She recited what she knew was engraved on the piece of pale glass showing half a foot and some elegant toes. '"S.C. These three will abide. 1919."'

'"These three will abide"?'

She smiled softly to herself. 'It's about One Corinthians, Thirteen, I think. A favourite at weddings.' She looked around the room. 'I wish I had a Bible to check it out, though. Don't happen to have one to hand, do you?'

He shook his head. 'But I know a place nearby where we can lay hands on one.'

Faith stopped to look at the window in the chapel while Marcus rummaged in the tiny cluttered vestry for a Bible. Even with her knees and lower legs missing, and the bottom section of the window boarded up, the woman captured in stained glass was exquisite.

The expression on her upturned face was pure rapture. All around her flowers bloomed—daisies in the grass, roses beside her in the bushes, climbing ivy above her head, reaching for the stars in the night sky. Faith could see why Crowbridge hadn't been able to give up on the idea of making his vision come to life, no matter what the medium.

Marcus returned from the vestry with a worn black leather Bible and began to hunt through it. While he was occupied leafing through the tissue-thin pages, Faith allowed herself to do what she normally resisted—let her eyes rove over him. How was it fair for a man to be so beautiful?

Finally he placed a long finger in the centre of a page and smiled before looking up at her.

This time when their eyes met she didn't get that earth-shifting-on-its-axis sensation. No, this was much more subtle, and probably much more dangerous. She felt a slow slipping, like the motion of a sled at the top of a snow-covered hill as gravity got hold and it started to move. Once it gathered momentum there'd be no stopping it.

He read out a verse, and the old-fashioned language of the King James Version sat well on his tongue. "'For now we see through a glass, darkly; but then face to face: now I know in part; but then shall I know even as also I am known.'"

Faith's heart skipped a beat in the pause before he moved on to the next verse.

Know even as also I am known...

She felt as if those words had been waiting all those centuries for here and now—for her and the man reading them to her. Because that was how she felt with him: she knew him, even though they'd only met just over a fortnight ago. How was that possible?

Everyone else, even her family—especially her family—looked at her through tinted glass, only getting glimpses, never seeing or understanding the whole. Somehow this man managed to do what no one else could. But she liked her tinted glass, liked her separateness. At least she had up until now.

'It's the next one,' she said. 'Read the next one.'

He looked down again. "'And now abideth faith, hope, charity, these three; but the greatest of these is charity.'"

She blew out a breath. *These three will abide.* 'That reference makes it even more sure. He was finishing his trio of pictures. The other two weren't complete without this one.'

A sharp pang deep inside her chest cavity caused her to fall silent. That was how she and Hope and Grace had been once upon a time—the terrible trio, Gram had used to call them, with a glimmer in her eyes that was reserved only for grandparents. But they hadn't been that way for a long time, and Faith suddenly missed them terribly, even though she hadn't let herself feel that way in years.

If only she could believe that, just like Crowbridge's pictures, her sisters weren't complete without her. But the truth was that they and Mom and Dad were fully related to each other, were a complete family unit on their own; she only had one foot in and one foot out. A cuckoo. One who didn't fit in, who shouldn't even try.

'That's good, then,' Marcus said beside her.

He was closer now, within touching distance. He could reach for her if he wanted to. And she sensed he did. She closed her eyes and walked away, saw the open door of the vestry and headed towards it. She needed distance, space. Because letting Marcus take care of her, look out for her, even for just a few moments, was almost as dumb as going to the ball that evening. She couldn't let herself get sucked into this vision of a fairy tale—this place, this man. The ball always ended badly for Cinderella, so she'd much rather be Rapunzel, safe in her turret...

No, she meant *tower*. Safe in her tower.

She entered and discovered where most of the debris from

the tidy chapel had ended up. It was like the cellar all over again.

Bad idea. She didn't need reminders of the cellar right now. Or, to be more precise, of what had happened in the cellar.

She turned to go, but Marcus was already blocking the door, watching her. She glanced around frantically, looking for something to distract her, to start a conversation. There was a pile of old papers on the desk. She picked them up. On top was a note from the clean-up crew leader.

Found these in a trunk up in the tower. Thought someone might want to look through them.

'I don't believe it,' she muttered. 'Clear up one dusty dumping ground and then someone finds another one to be dealt with.' She handed him the papers. 'Sorry, Your Lordship, but this bunch is all yours.'

He took it from her after giving her a small salute. That made her smile. While he leafed through the papers, many of them torn or mildewed, Faith wandered out to look at the window once again. He followed, still flicking through the stack.

'Look…' He pulled a faded and yellowing piece out of the pile. 'Someone else has done a sketch of the window.'

She walked over and took the piece from his hands, mildly interested. Even folded into quarters Faith recognised the pattern of lines. She'd been working with them all week. But when she unfolded it her hand flew to cover her mouth.

'What?' he said. 'What is it?'

She shook her head, an expression of total disbelief on her face. Her mouth moved once or twice but no sound came out.

'Faith?'

She held up a hand and took a deep breath. 'Marcus, this is the *cartoon!*'

He frowned, and she knew he was thinking of comic books and kids' TV shows.

'The original drawing that the glaziers worked from!' she explained as she turned it round in her hands and checked the corners and edges. 'Yes! Look, there's his signature—Samuel Crowbridge!'

Marcus squinted at the drawing, but he hardly had time to focus on it before she danced away with it, spinning round and then running to the window to hold it up and compare.

'That's two pieces of evidence in one day!' she yelled over her shoulder. It was more than she could ever have hoped for.

But then she stopped smiling, stopped talking, and her eyes grew wide again. She ducked down and spread the cartoon on the floor, smoothing it out gently. She was staring at the drawing, but her brain was refusing to compute. It kept telling her eyes the information they were sending it was wrong. *Return to sender.*

Marcus walked over and stood behind her to take a look.

And so he should. Right at the bottom, roughly where the rectangle they'd been discussing earlier was, were some words. She looked up at him.

'This isn't in the window now. Somebody changed it.' She lowered her voice to barely a whisper. 'Somebody *took it out.*'

Marcus wasn't moving. His eyes were blinking and his mouth was slightly open. '"Proverbs Four, Verse Eighteen,"' he finally read, his voice hoarse. 'Why would someone want to take that out?'

Faith swallowed. 'Because to someone it meant something.'

But that would make it… That would make it…

'Bertie was right after all,' she said, looking up at him. 'Once upon a time there was a message in this window.'

CHAPTER EIGHT

'PROVERBS, Chapter Four, Verse eighteen...' Faith couldn't help muttering it to herself over and over as she got dressed. A message in the window? Maybe. But a very cryptic one.

She left an earring hanging in her ear without its back so she could go and pull the piece of paper she'd scribbled the verse on out of her purse.

'"But the path of the just is as a shining light, that shineth more and more unto the perfect day",' she read out loud.

Beautiful poetry, nice sentiment, but was this the kind of message a husband would send his wife? It seemed Bertie's message in the window asked more questions than it answered.

She put the piece of paper on the nightstand and went back to getting ready. In a moment of weakness, of sheer jubilation, after finding two bits of proof that were going to put her name on the academic map, she'd relented and agreed to go to the Christmas Ball. Bertie had rubbed his hands together when he'd heard the news, and had insisted escorting her personally to a bedroom with a wardrobe stuffed with evening gowns. Another sign that hoarding went hand in hand with the Huntington genes, she guessed.

She'd chosen a red velvet dress from the early sixties, with a scooped neck and tight bodice that skimmed her hips and then flared into a full fishtail at the bottom. It was gorgeous.

Maybe a little snug, but gorgeous. Bertie had also insisted she borrow a necklace that he'd retrieved from a walnut jewellery box on the dressing table. She touched the simple V of glittering stones with her fingertips. My, she hoped they were paste.

Before she lost the matching earrings, she returned to the dresser and pushed the missing back on. The only thing to do before taking her first good look at herself in the mirror was to put on the pair of long red gloves that had been stored with the dress. She put them on slowly, avoiding the moment she had to meet her own eyes in the full-length glass.

When she had the courage to look it was as bad as she'd feared.

Not only did she look stunning, and the dress fitted like a second skin, but she had that kind of glow in her eyes a woman only got when she was halfway to falling in love.

Disaster.

She'd hoped that when she saw herself in the mirror everything would look wrong—that she'd look as if she was playing dress-up. It would be so much easier to remember that she didn't belong, that she shouldn't want to. Instead she looked like a princess. It was disgusting.

You can't want him, she told herself. He's not for you. If you didn't fit in in plain old Beckett's Run, how on earth do you think you're going to fit in here?

But she'd promised Bertie she would attend the ball, even dance with him, so she couldn't back out.

She took one last glance at herself in the mirror. *Stop sparkling,* she told her eyes. *You have no business to be doing that.* And then she took in a deep breath, held it for a few seconds and headed for the door.

The ball was already well underway when Faith made her way down the main staircase. She deliberately left it until late, hoping minimum exposure to all the glitz and glamour might help her stay strong.

She couldn't have been more wrong.

She should have come down earlier. Because she needed this. Needed the slap in the face it gave her when she walked down the stairs.

Even though she'd only been here a week or two, somehow she'd got comfortable with Hadsborough—with its little yellow drawing room and her quirky turret bedroom. Here, from her spot on the first landing, before the marble steps disappeared into a throng of people, she was once again confronted with the reality of this place.

It wasn't an ordinary home. It was a castle. And it had never looked more like one than it did tonight. Candles were everywhere, their flickering light taking the evening back into a bygone age. Glasses clinked, champagne fizzed, while guests in tuxedos and ballgowns milled and danced. The Beckett's Run definition of a 'relaxed' dress code was obviously very different from the Hadsborough one. Every single guest was dressed up to the nines and loving it.

Faith might as well have come down the staircase and stepped on the surface of Mars. It would have been just as familiar. She was used to home cooking and takeout, town festivals and barn dances. Parties where people drank to forget their daily life, not because they were partaking in some kind of fantasy.

And in the middle of it all was Marcus, looking elegant in bow tie and crisp white shirt, his dark suit screaming Savile Row tailoring. Her knees literally started to wobble. He looked so handsome, with his dark hair flopping slightly over his forehead, a small frown creasing his brow as he listened intently to an older woman in a tiara.

A tiara. This was the kind of shebang where people wore tiaras. Real ones.

Her fingers traced the necklace and she wished fervently there was a safe she could put it in somewhere. The last time Faith had worn a tiara she'd been seven years old, and it had

been made of silver-coated plastic, with garish pink gems
stuck on the front.

She shouldn't have agreed to come. She'd known this was
a bad idea.

But there was Bertie at the bottom of the stairs, smiling
up at her and holding out his arm. She swallowed her nerves
and started to walk down the stairs.

Fake it, she reminded herself. *You know you look the part,
even if it's just window dressing. It's like yawning or laughing.
You start off forcing it and after a while it comes naturally.*

She glanced over in Marcus's direction as she reached the
bottom step. He was still deep in conversation with Tiara
Woman and, on the pretence of needing a drink, she took
Bertie's arm and neatly steered him the other direction. The
only way she was going to survive this evening was if she
kept out of Marcus's way.

There was a flash of red at the corner of Marcus's eye. He
didn't know why he turned towards it. When his eyes had
focused on it properly, however, he fully understood why his
jaw had dropped and his throat had tightened.

Wow.

Faith was on the other side of the room, in a red velvet
dress that clung to every inch of her slender frame. He'd
known her slim lines and understated curves appealed to him
in jeans and a sweater, but tonight…

And then she turned round, revealing a low-cut back to
the demure-fronted dress that made him realise he might be
an earl but he was also part caveman.

She was talking to someone, smiling broadly and using
hand gestures. He knew when she realised he was looking
at her because she suddenly went still. A second later she
twisted round to meet his gaze. Above her crimson lips was
a pair of large, questioning eyes. The problem was his brain

was so fried by the sight of her in that dress that he had no idea what the question was, let alone the answer.

He'd always thought her beautiful, right from that first day in the chapel, when he'd seen her studying the window, her face aglow with its colour. But here, tonight, in that dress, looking as if she was made for it, he couldn't help wondering if he should stop fighting that feeling that she was made for him.

He didn't know what to do about that.

Especially as he'd promised her he'd keep his distance.

Especially as he'd promised *himself* he wouldn't forget his own sensible plans for the next woman in his life.

But part of him ached to make the jump anyway, to give whatever was simmering between them a chance. However, the part that had been burned by Amanda's departure was backing off fast, shaking its head. Hadn't he'd thought Amanda the perfect fit too? On paper, much more so than Faith. He had to give Amanda her dues—she'd stuck with him a full six months after his father's death before she'd finally jumped ship.

That had stung. In his own charge-the-world-head-on way he'd still been grieving. He'd needed her understanding, not his spare keys in his palm and a kiss on the cheek. He'd thought she was the one person in the world he could rely on. And he'd been wrong. It didn't help to know that Faith McKinnon was a hundred times more skittish.

Even so, he excused himself from the conversation he'd been having and walked towards her, not taking his eyes from her face. He saw her heave in a breath, saw her eyes grow wide, knew the exact moment she'd decided to run but found her feet glued to the floor. It gave him a flash of male pride to know she reacted to him that way, that he wasn't the only one in its grip.

He could make her change her mind if he wanted to.

He knew that. And, oh, how he wanted to. But he'd given his word.

Nothing to say they couldn't have a platonic dance, though. Especially at a big Christmas party like this. It was practically expected.

He reached her and opened his arms. She placed one gloved hand in his and the other slid to his shoulder, leaving his left hand to rest on her shoulderblade, touching delicious bare skin. Wordlessly they started to dance, moving through the chatting guests until they joined more couples on the dance floor.

Marcus hardly noticed who else was there, waltzing with them. He wasn't really aware of doing anything—not moving his arms or legs, not dodging the other couples, just looking down at Faith, with some silent conversation going on between them.

He wished that duty and decency hadn't been drummed into him since he was in nappies. Wished he could say *what the hell* and sweep her into his arms, drag her under the large bunch of mistletoe hanging from the chandelier over the dance floor and kiss her senseless in front of all these people. Suddenly he was slightly irritated with her for making him promise, because he couldn't quite bring himself to steamroll over her feelings and take what he wanted as easily as he'd like to. That damn protective instinct of his kept him at bay.

That was why, when the music ended, he let her nod her thanks and slip from his arms, find another partner. Why he turned his back and did the same, refusing to watch her go.

But as he moved his feet to the rhythm of the music a thought started to pulse inside his head. Just for one night he wanted to ditch his blasted code of honour. He wished he could be wild and reckless and not care a bean about what the morning would bring. He'd hardly chosen a thing for himself in the last two years, always doing the right thing, always doing his duty, what was good for the family.

Tonight, for once, he wanted to choose something for himself. And he really wanted to choose Faith.

Faith had deliberately sought out the villagers of Hadsborough to talk to. She understood them, knew what they were about. And they were keen to chat about the restoration of the chapel and the stained glass window, keeping her busy, keeping her mind off where Marcus was and who he was with.

But after a couple of hours of being 'on', of having to smile and chat to one new person after another, Faith began to tire. In the back of her head she was still mulling over the puzzling Bible reference in the window, trying to work out if it meant something.

And when she wasn't trying to figure that out, and make small talk with the next person who asked her about the window, there was Marcus. Every time she caught sight of him she experienced a sudden stab of breathlessness.

'May I have another dance, my dear?'

She turned round to find Bertie beside her, smiling. He was in fine spirits this evening, and more energetic than she'd ever seen him.

'Of course, Your Grace,' she said, and offered him her hand.

Bertie shook his head as he took it and led her onto the dance floor. 'Time was when I'd have put on a good show for a pretty thing like you,' he said. 'I was quite the Fred Astaire in my day, I'll have you know.' He sighed. 'No more dips and turns for this old back any more, though. You'll have to put up with my shuffling instead.'

Faith laughed as Bertie took her in a classic ballroom hold. 'And very elegant shuffling it is, too.'

He smiled back at her. 'You'll have to get Marcus to give you another spin round the dance floor.'

She kept her expression neutral. 'You wouldn't be trying to matchmake, would you, Bertie?'

He shrugged. 'The boy needs to have more fun.'

Faith didn't say anything, just let him lead her round the dance floor. Slowly. She didn't disagree with Bertie, but whatever was going on between her and his grandson definitely wasn't fun. It felt more like torture.

The music changed, and Bertie bowed to her and took his leave. Faith tried to curtsey back, but she wobbled badly in her borrowed shoes. A warm hand at her elbow steadied her. She turned to find herself staring up into a pair of smoky blue eyes.

'Hi,' she said softly.

His lips curved upwards. 'Hi.'

And just like that her last defence fell. She'd thought it was made of cast iron, but sadly it snapped like spun sugar. The band were playing a slow number and she ended up with her head on his shoulder, one arm looped around his neck.

Try not to notice, she told herself. Try not to notice how well your head fits in the space near his neck, or how your bodies slot together like jigsaw pieces. Or how your chests rise and fall together, even when you're not trying to match rhythm.

To distract herself she started thinking about the verse in the cartoon—the one that could be the key to Bertie's past. Why hide it if it wasn't? Why would someone have gone to all that trouble if the verse had nothing to do with the story Bertie had heard about his mother? And did the numbers have significance? Or was it in the words of the verse themselves?

'Proverbs Four-Eighteen?' he whispered in her ear.

She lifted her head and looked him in the eye. 'How did you know?'

He shook his head, a rueful expression on his face.

'What do you think the verse means? Have you had any thoughts?'

He pressed his lips together, then said, 'Plenty of thoughts. Not sure any of them lead anywhere.'

Faith breathed out a little. This was easier, safer. They needed to keep talking about the window.

Marcus frowned as he pulled up a memory. 'My great uncle told me once that his brother was very fond of treasure hunts. He used to lay one out every Christmas in the grounds for the village children.'

Faith's eyes grew wide. 'So maybe the reference isn't a message in itself but a clue to something else? Another verse? Another destination?'

'We should look for key words,' he said.

'Path,' she said, nodding to herself.

'And shining light,' they both said, at exactly the same time, then both looked away and back again in complete synchronisation.

'Stop doing that,' she said. 'It's freaking me out.'

A mischievous glint appeared in Marcus's eye. 'It's not just me.' Then his expression became thoughtful. 'There are paths all over the estate, but we don't even know if it refers to something literal or figurative. As for shining lights…'

She closed her eyes, attempted to visualise the parts of the grounds she had visited. Shining light…

Her lids flipped open. 'How about that grandfather clock in the cellar? That has a sun on it.'

'Maybe…' He didn't look convinced. 'But if this is a clue leading to something else there should be something there to find—some more writing or another verse. Like a treasure trail. We had a good look at that clock and I didn't see anything like that.'

They'd still been swaying to the music as they'd been talking, but suddenly Marcus went completely still.

'Of course…' he said on an out-breath. 'I've been so stupid not have seen it!'

And then he went quiet again.

Faith punched him on the chest softly. 'Marcus!'

He blinked and looked down at her. She gave him a look

that said she might have to hurt him if he didn't spill the beans.

He laughed loudly enough to make some of the other dancing couples close to them look their way, then stepped back, grabbed her hand and pulled her in the direction of the door.

'I know where there are both paths and a shining light,' he said, picking up speed.

Once they were out of the ballroom he guided her towards the front door.

'Marcus! I have heels on.'

He gave her a blank look.

'And it's been snowing outside! I want to solve the mystery as much as you do, but I'd rather not get frostbitten toes doing it.'

He nodded and changed direction, heading for the small staircase that led to the kitchens. They ran right through and to the back door.

'Here,' he said, and threw a padded coat to her. Once she had it on over her dress he nudged a pair of Wellington boots her way. 'They're Shirley's,' he said, 'and she always keeps a spare pair of socks inside.'

While she kicked off her heels and sank her feet into the boots, which were at least a size too big, he pulled a coat off the row of pegs and shoved his feet into his own boots.

Then the back door was open and icy air was chilling their cheeks. Marcus grabbed her hand and pulled her out into the moonlit night.

There was something thrilling about running out of the castle with Marcus on this snowy night, her skirts caught up in her free hand, not knowing where she was going. The paths round the estate were mostly cleared, and they kept to them as much as possible. Faith kept lagging behind, caught up in staring at the formal gardens and the rolling fields beyond, all sparkling in the moonlight as if someone had dusted them with glitter, but the insistent tug of Marcus's hand in hers kept her travelling.

'Where are we going?' she asked, frowning slightly. For some reason she'd thought they might end up at the chapel, but they were jogging in the opposite direction.

He turned to grin wolfishly at her. 'We're almost there.'

She looked around. High yew hedges ran alongside the path they were running on. She didn't think she'd ventured into this part of the estate before—too busy stuck in her studio bent over bits of glass to notice what had been right under her nose.

They kept running until they came upon a gap in the hedge, closed off by an iron gate. Marcus stopped and lifted the latch, making sure he still had her by the hand.

'There are plenty of paths here,' he said softly, 'but only one is the right one. Only one winds upwards towards a shining light.'

As he led her through the gate suddenly it all made sense.

'You have a maze,' she mumbled, slightly awestruck.

'They were the craze in Victorian times. The fourth Duke had it planted, but my great-grandfather added some improvements.'

She looked up to where the hedges ended, about two feet above her head. A couple of inches of snow glistened on top, pale blue in the moonlight, making the whole maze look like a rather elaborately carved Christmas cake.

'We're going to try to navigate a maze in the dark, in the snow?' she asked, realising she sounded disbelieving.

Marcus just laughed. He pulled a flashlight from his pocket and handed it to her. 'Do you want to race me to the centre or do you want to do it together?'

She narrowed her eyes at him. 'And you're giving *me* the only light source?'

He nodded.

'I have a feeling you know your way through this maze

even in the pitch-dark, which would be cheating, so I'm sticking with you.'

She was rewarded with a broad grin at that comment. 'Smart lady,' he murmured, and then tugged her off to the right and started running again—just as her heart decided to lurch along in an uneven rhythm, making it even harder for her to keep up.

After a while Faith gave up trying to memorise their path. She just concentrated on keeping her skirt off the ground and matching Marcus's pace. When she stumbled slightly he turned, looking concerned.

'Am I going too fast for you?'

She nodded, panting slightly. 'These boots are a bit flappy, and I really don't want to ruin this lovely dress. This skirt wasn't made for running.'

He looked her up and down, a thoughtful look on his face, taking in the fishtail skirt, how it kept her thighs so close together. Feeling his gaze on her body made said thighs tingle. She told herself if was just the cold.

'Only one solution to that,' he said, and stepped towards her.

She gasped as he lifted her into his arms. Instinctively she looped her arms round his neck and held on tight. 'What are you doing?' she asked, her voice breathy. 'You can't possibly carry me the rest of the way like this!'

'Would you prefer a fireman's lift?' he replied, a ripple of humour in his voice.

She shook her head violently, thinking how the blood would rush to her head if he hoisted her over his shoulder. She was finding it difficult enough to think as it was.

'Are you flirting with me, Lord Westerham?' she asked shakily. 'Because I thought we had an agreement about that sort of thing.'

'Of course not,' he said, with a slightly devilish glint in his eye. And as he started to walk he added. 'Pity, though. That would have been a great view.'

She slapped him on the chest with a gloved hand. 'Earls are not supposed to talk like that.'

He just smiled a secret smile to himself, staring straight ahead, navigating the maze. 'I beg to differ. I've known quite a few, and I know from experience that a title is not a ticket to a clean mouth. Far from it. You should hear Ashford when he gets going…'

She slapped him again. 'You're teasing me.'

He slowed and looked down at her. 'Maybe I am. But don't let the title fool you. I might be an earl, but underneath I'm still a man.'

The glitter in his eyes as he looked down at her bore witness to that. Faith found herself strangely breathless. Wrenching her gaze onto the path ahead was difficult, but she managed it.

He picked up speed, staying silent, but his last words thrummed between them still. Yes, he was a man. A beautiful, noble man. And right at this moment, captured in his arms as she was, Faith McKinnon was feeling very much a woman. Even worse, that woman was doing just as he asked, and was forgetting all about his title and why she shouldn't just drop her gift-wrapped heart at his feet like a tiny Christmas present.

She hung on, closing her eyes.

Sooner than expected he came to a halt and slowly lowered her to the ground. Cold air rushed in between them, where their bodies had been pressed against each other. Faith shivered.

'See what I mean?' he whispered, his breath warm in her frozen ear.

She blinked and looked around. This wasn't what she'd expected. In front of them was a squat tower of stone, sloping inwards slightly as it rose maybe fifteen feet into the air.

'Come on,' Marcus said, and reached for her hand.

This time she took it without thinking. It seemed to belong there.

'We're near the end of a path that leads to a shining light.'

He led her round the stone mound until they came upon a narrow winding stairway that circled the tower. It didn't take long to climb up the twenty or so stairs, and soon they were standing on a viewing platform, surrounded by waist-high stone walls. She could not only see the whole of the snow-capped maze, but also the hills beyond, and glittering in the distance the larger of the two lakes.

The moon was in evidence, but no other light was anywhere to be seen. 'Where—?'

He placed a hand on each of her shoulders and gently turned her to face the other direction. There, in the middle of the tower, was a sundial mounted on a stone pedestal.

She walked towards it and his hands slid off her shoulders. However, they didn't drop away quickly, but trailed down her back until she was out of reach. Even through the puffy layers of Shirley's winter coat she could feel warmth, the sure pressure of his hands.

'How do you know this is what the verse is referring to? The connection seems a bit tenuous.' As wonderfully romantic as this idea was, she couldn't help think it might just be a coincidence.

'It would be but for two reasons,' he said, coming to the other side of the sundial and standing opposite her. 'First, the same man who commissioned the window also built this tower in the maze. Second...' He tapped the brass face of the sundial with a finger, before lifting up the flashlight and shining it down on it.

There, at the base of the clockface, was an inscription.

'Song Twenty-Two?' she said. 'I don't get it.'

'I think it's another Bible reference. That's why when I thought of paths and shining lights and the need for an-

other piece of the puzzle this place popped into my mind.'
He walked round the sundial to stand next to her. 'Song, I
think, is short for Song of Solomon, or Song of Songs, and
if you look carefully there, between the twos, it's a colon.'

'Song of Songs, Chapter Two, Verse Two?' she asked, her
voice barely a whisper.

He nodded.

She turned to face him, did her best to read his face in the
semi-darkness. 'You think there's something in this?'

He stared back at her and breathed out hard. 'Maybe. If it
was any of these things on their own I'd probably dismiss it,
but put them all together...'

'What about Bertie? You were really worried this would
upset him. It still might.'

His eyelids lowered briefly and he looked away. 'I know.
But if what my family has told him all these years is wrong,
he has a right to know.' Marcus looked back at her. 'I've been
trying to protect him from a lie, but I don't think it's right to
protect him from the truth.'

She saw it—the twist of guilt in his face as the dual needs
both to keep his grandfather safe and to do the right thing
warred inside him.

'The truth comes out sooner or later,' she said. 'I wish...'

She closed her eyes. She had been about to say that she
wished her parents had told her who her real father was earlier, but she suddenly realised how cruel that would have
been. There had been no easy way to handle it, had there?
Telling an eight-year-old something like that would have been
devastating. Although not telling her had wreaked its own
kind of havoc. Suddenly she understood why her mother
had swept it all under the carpet and pretended it had nothing to do with her, why she still seemed so blasé about the
whole thing.

Seeing the tortured look in Marcus's eyes a moment ago
made her ache deep inside. She wished just one of the adults

involved in the fiasco of her birth had felt that burning urge to protect *her* that way, instead of abandoning her—either physically or emotionally.

She opened her eyes and looked up at Marcus, knowing he would do the right thing no matter the cost to himself. He was that kind of man. Something deep down in Faith's soul broke free and reached for him, and where her mind went her hands followed.

It didn't have to be for ever, did it? She knew she didn't belong with him long-term. But that didn't mean she couldn't have him just for now. Why was she stopping herself?

Take it, Faith. Take something for yourself for once, instead of running away from everything.

It was only just over a week until the Carol Service, and after that she'd be gone. At least she'd have a cool story to tell—or hide from—her grandkids one day. *I once had a fling with an earl...*

She reached up and touched his cheek. Her eyes were suddenly moist and threatening to produce a black, streaky waterfall down her face. She stepped forward, put a trembling hand on his chest. He stiffened, and she knew he was doing as he'd promised, holding himself back because he'd given his word.

The only problem was she didn't want him to hold back any more.

'Faith McKinnon, are you flirting with me?' His voice was raw, despite the levity of his words. 'I thought we had an agreement.'

Faith's heart pounded so hard she thought it might knock her over. She knew she was about to cross a boundary that she herself had put in place, that the resulting fall-out could be blamed on no one else. But just for once she wanted to feel as if she wasn't alone, an outsider.

'No, I'm not flirting with you, Marcus,' she said, her voice husky as she reached up and hooked her hand round his neck to pull him closer. 'I'm kissing you.'

CHAPTER NINE

THIS was no soft, exploratory, getting-to-know-you kiss, Marcus realised. They were way past that. It was as if he already knew her this way. He could anticipate just when and where she was going to move her hands, knew just when the next breathy sigh was coming. They couldn't have been more in synch with each other if they'd been lovers for years. And if he hadn't been wearing Wellington boots she'd have blown his big old woolly socks off!

He dipped his hands inside her half-open coat, finding her tightly corseted waist inside the bodice of her dress, feeling the velvet rasp against the pads of his fingers as he pulled close. In response she buried her hands inside his hair and pressed herself against him. Faith McKinnon hadn't uttered a word, but that hadn't stopped her being as direct as usual about what she wanted from him.

That thought both set his toes on fire and stopped him cold at the same time. It took all he had to gently pull away, to disentangle himself from her. She moaned in protest as he dragged his lips from hers, and that was almost his undoing. Almost. He pulled back and held her face between his hands.

'Faith…'

Her lids were still closed and she let out a frustrated sigh. 'Don't be noble, Marcus. Just kiss me again.'

He obliged—a short, hot kiss that he was only just able to

control. 'We can't stay out here,' he murmured. 'You'll die of hypothermia.'

She opened her eyes and looked straight at him. Straight *through* him, it felt like. Her pupils were huge and he felt their tug like a giant magnet.

Her voice was low and oh-so-sexy as she said, 'Then take me back inside.'

He didn't have to ask what she meant. He almost growled in frustration. This wasn't a different-bed-every-night woman; something deep inside told him that. It also told him that she wasn't one to give all she had easily, that she didn't let that many people close. The caveman part of him rose up and cheered at the thought he wouldn't be the last in a long, long line of lovers. The Earl, however—damn him—had other ideas.

He stepped back, but kept one arm around her and led her down the short curling staircase that circled the mound.

She shivered against him. Whether from the promise of further heat or the cold night air he didn't know.

'Please tell me it's not going to take as long to get out as it did to get in. Forget hypothermia! I think I might just expire from frustration.'

'It's not going to take as long,' he said, and guided her further round the mound. After a short break the steps continued curling, but this time underground, leading them under the stone tower and under the maze.

'Oh, wow!' she said as they descended into a small grotto under the centre of the maze. The stone walls were lined with shells of different shapes and sizes, and a small fountain dribbled into a pool at one edge of the chamber.

She grabbed his arm and pulled herself tightly into his side as they passed through the grotto, down another short flight of curving stairs, and then along a winding shell-lined path, created to mimic a limestone cave with stalactites and stalagmites. At the end was an iron gate and another flight of stairs that took them out onto a different side of the maze from where they'd entered.

Faith punched him on the arm. 'You mean we could have just got in that way all along!'

Despite his sudden serious mood he felt his lips curl up at the edges. 'It wouldn't have been half as much fun.'

She looked as if she was going to argue, but then her expression softened. She pressed her lips softly against his. 'No,' she mumbled against his mouth between kisses. 'Maybe it wouldn't have.'

He looked at the path in front of them, and then down at Faith's beautiful red dress, already wet round the hem. He knew she'd be horrified if she thought she'd ruined it, even though Bertie wouldn't give a fig.

Also, there was only one way he could come up with to stop himself doing something they might both regret in the morning. So while she was distracted, looking out over the gently sloping lawn that ran between the maze and the lower lake, he bent down, grabbed her round the thighs and threw her over his shoulder.

'Marcus!' she squealed. 'Put…me…down!'

'This is for your own good,' he muttered through clenched teeth, and started walking.

She pounded on his back for a few steps. 'You're an insufferable tyrant, do you know that?' she said from somewhere behind him, but her arms circled his chest to steady herself.

'I've been told it runs in the family,' he said, a grin forming on his lips. Maybe he was a little twisted, but he was starting to enjoy himself. And he needed to keep this light, needed to keep it breezy. 'And, Faith…?'

'What?'

She sounded more than a little disgruntled. Too bad.

'I was right about the view.'

* * *

Faith had never been so glad to see a kitchen door in her life. Despite her repeated pleadings Marcus had carried her all the way back to the castle hoisted over his shoulder. When she'd complained that the guests must be leaving the ball by now, and someone might see them, he'd just taken a back route, using a path than ran past the cellar windows.

However, maybe the blood rushing to her head had done her some good. Bizarrely, she was thinking straighter now it was back where it should be, rather than making other body parts thrum with longing.

That didn't mean she regretted what she'd asked him, just that she understood why he'd held back. This would be a big deal, not some quick tumble in the haystack. Was she really ready for all that would mean, both good and bad?

On the one hand it would be a wonderful, wonderful affair. On the other… She could end up falling all the way in love with him, and then she'd really be in trouble. She didn't know which would be worse—having him and losing him, or never knowing what it would be like, always wishing she'd taken the chance when she had it.

As they entered the kitchen he skilfully managed to deposit her the right way up without making her feel like a sack of potatoes.

'Marcus…' she whispered.

He looked impossibly sexy, with his hair all messed up and his eyes all dark and serious.

He threaded his fingers through hers. 'Come.'

Her blood started heading in all the wrong directions again at the hint of promise in the word. They went up the staircase to the ground floor proper, and then through a network of corridors and rooms until they ended up in the most beautiful library. Marcus turned a single lamp on, and its glow bathed that corner of the room in warm yellow light.

On every available stretch of wall that wasn't occupied by either a door or a fireplace there were huge ornately carved bookshelves, most groaning with the weight of leather-bound books. But instead of the wood having a dark varnish, the whole room was painted a soft buttery cream. There were three peacock-coloured damask-covered sofas—one L-shaped to fit in front of the only corner bookcase. Marcus motioned for her to sit down.

He pulled a book from the shelf and came to join her on the corner sofa. He opened the book, leafed through to find a place and handed it to her.

Song of Songs.

She shot him a look and then focused on the page.

'What does it say?' he asked.

Faith skimmed down the whole of the first chapter, getting a feel for the context, before turning the page over and finding the second and reading from verse one. '"I am the rose of Sharon, and the lily of the valleys."' She looked up. 'Rose of Sharon! Just like in the window. This *has* to be connected.' She looked down again and carried on to the second verse: '"As the lily among thorns, so is my love among the daughters."' She met his gaze again. 'Well, that's an obvious declaration of love, I guess.'

He nodded, but he didn't look down at the book in her hands, just at her. She swallowed. All her life she'd felt like a thorn—something that got in other people's way, snagged them when they wanted to be free—but when he looked at her like that she felt as fragile and as elegant as a lily. With a rush of understanding, she suddenly understood just how remarkable those words were. What an amazing thing it was to be longed for like that, to be adored rather than merely tolerated.

She continued reading. It was beautiful. Not a sermon, or a fire and brimstone prophecy, but a poem—a declaration between two lovers, full of evocative words and sensual imagery. The man who'd used a verse from this to send a message to his wife had definitely not thought he'd made a mistake in marrying her. Far from it.

She glanced over the text again. "'Do not stir up or awaken love until it pleases…" What do you think that means?'

He leaned forward and looked at her intently. 'Maybe that there's a right time and a wrong time for everything—even love?'

She gave a huff. 'I think my mother's living proof of that. She's always falling in love with something, or someone, or some place. It always ends in disaster… It's not that she hasn't got a big heart—quite the reverse. She always gives away too much, and always too soon.' She paused and looked at the text again. '*Until it pleases*… Maybe that's the answer—her timing sucks.'

He threaded his fingers together, balancing his elbows on his knees, and looked into her eyes. 'I don't think she's alone in that. Love seems to have more casualties than it does success stories.'

She knew what he was saying, could almost see into a future where they were both limping away from each other, in much worse shape than they were now.

She exhaled loudly. 'And what about us, Marcus? Is it the right time or the wrong time for us? How do we tell?'

'I don't know…' He sat up again and ran a hand through his hair. 'But I know it's something I couldn't walk away from after just one night.'

She nodded. Her heart felt like a stone, sinking inside her chest.

There was the answer to her earlier question. And she'd wanted so much to pretend she was one of those girls who could just fall into bed with a hot man and then fall out again the next morning without a backwards glance. Why did it have to be all or nothing with her? And why did she always end up on the *nothing* side of the equation?

He reached for her, tugged her hand and brought her to sit next to him. He pressed the most delicate of kisses to her temple and then left his lips there, as if he couldn't quite bring himself to move away.

All or nothing.

What had grown already was too much to brush off as a flirtation, or rebrand and cheapen as a fling. They were hovering at a threshold, and she was too scared to cross it.

One step. Not even a leap. That was all it was.

But that one step would change everything.

The light seeping through the crack in the drawn curtains was cold and grey. Faith stirred against him. Marcus wasn't sure if he'd been dozing or not. It only seemed seconds ago that his mind had been whirring between the window, the mysterious verses and the woman nestled against him.

His arm was stretched along the back of the blue sofa cushions and Faith, still in her red ballgown and Shirley's borrowed coat, was burrowed into his side, her cheek on one side of her chest and her palm splayed possessively above his heart. He bowed his head and pressed a silent kiss to her silky hair. She moved again, just enough to signal she was on her way to consciousness.

Marcus closed his eyes and let the back of his skull rest against the sofa cushions. Even though he was cold and stiff, and his right leg was numb, he wished this night could have just dragged on and on. He hadn't quite finished relishing the feel of her curled against him, her rhythmic breathing warming his shirt. There was no way of knowing if he'd ever get the chance to have her soft and sleeping against him again, so he was wringing every second he could from the moment.

She wouldn't want to burrow so close against him if she knew what a coward he was.

Noble? *Don't think so.*

Running scared? *Oh, yes.*

He'd done a lot of thinking in the grey hours of the night. Saying no to Faith last night had been a gut reaction. He'd even managed to kid himself he'd been doing it for *her* benefit.

He was such a liar.

There was one reason and one reason alone that had held him back: fear. Nothing very noble about that.

The same strange perception that let him eavesdrop on her thoughts, anticipate her kisses, had told him something else. Something that had sent him running like a frightened deer. He knew without a shadow of a doubt that if he'd spent the night with Faith this morning he'd have been so besotted he'd have lain his heart at her feet—like some sappy knight of old who risked everything just for a wave of his lady's handkerchief.

So, as amazing as a night with Faith would be, he wasn't sure he could afford the cost.

She made a sleepy noise and used the hand on his chest to lever herself up and look him in the face.

'I feel like crap,' she said, and he couldn't help but laugh.

He brushed a wonky tendril that had escaped her pinned-up hairdo behind her ear. She didn't sugarcoat her words for anyone, did she?

She yawned, then fixed him with a steady gaze. 'What now?'

He knew her question had many layers. He decided to deal with the one he had an answer to. 'I spent a lot of time thinking last night and—aside from working out whether this new verse is a clue or just a coincidence, I thought it might be a good idea to find out more about my great-grandmother— Evangeline Huntington: the woman who started it all.'

She pushed herself away from him, so she could sit up straight, and pulled the puffy coat tighter around her. 'I didn't think your family talked about her. And they've done a hell of a job erasing any trace of her from Hadsborough.'

He nodded. 'But my family aren't the only ones who lived here, saw things. An army of servants have worked at the castle over the years, and if there's one thing that servants like to do it's gossip. Someone has to have heard something.'

She covered her mouth with her hand as another yawn escaped. 'You think the man who told you about the cellar might know something?'

'He's a good place to start.'

She looked down at her dress. It was creased horribly, and the Wellington boots were only half on, hanging off her feet. 'I'm not going anywhere like this.'

He stood up, caught her hands in his and pulled her up to meet him. She sighed as her feet dropped back into the boots with a sucking noise, and when she met his gaze he knew those other layers of questions were swirling round her head.

'Marcus? About us…?'

He shook his head. 'I don't know,' he said softly, and then he bent his head and tasted her lips one more time. He knew he shouldn't, but he just couldn't stop himself.

A week was all they had. If they'd had months ahead of them, if Faith had been going to settle down in one place for any length of time, then it might have been different. But he wasn't ready to jump right in. He had to be sure this time.

You are sure, a little voice said inside his head. *You know.*

Perhaps. But he didn't trust that little voice. He'd listened to it before—about Amanda, who had said she'd stick by him no matter what. And when his father had promised him everything was fine, that the company was just experiencing a minor blip. He'd listened to that smooth, soothing voice before and it had cost him everything. So, no, he wasn't in a rush, and he didn't think he should be.

'Then until we know,' she said, her pupils expanding, 'I suggest we maintain the status quo.'

He knew it was stupid to pretend they wouldn't get sucked in deeper, but he wasn't ready to let go just yet. One more week. That wasn't too much to ask, was it? Whatever was going on between them was balancing precariously, and it would fall one way or the other. And it would fall soon.

'A shower, a few hours' sleep and a good breakfast is in order before we do any more sleuthing,' he said, taking a step backwards.

Faith grabbed a hold of his shirt. 'Not so fast, buddy.' She used her grip to pull his face close to hers. 'I haven't finished with you just yet.'

Faith looked around her as she and Marcus walked through the terraced gardens beside the long lake.

'I don't suppose you know if there are any lilies under all that white stuff?' she asked him.

He shook his head. 'Even if I could remember it wouldn't matter. These gardens have been replanted and redesigned at least twice in the last thirty years alone. Even if that verse *is* a clue of some kind, we have to face the possibility that the lilies that were in the garden in my great-grandfather's day no longer exist.'

She sighed and stuffed her hand into her coat pocket. 'Well, let's hope this Mr Grey of yours has something enlightening to tell us.'

The walk across Hadsborough Park in the snow was gorgeous. Vast fields of white were still untouched by human feet, even though it had been days since the last snowfall and a fortnight since the first flakes.

The retired employee was visiting his son and daughter-in-law, who occupied a small stone cottage on the far edge of the estate, hewn from the same sandstone as the castle itself. Marcus used the knocker on the shiny red front door and they heard a faint voice call out from inside. He pushed the door and she followed him inside. They found Mr Grey sitting by the fire with a blanket over his knees. A middle-aged woman fussed around him, tucking it in. When she saw Marcus she stood up ramrod-straight and bobbed a quick curtsey.

'Morning, My Lord. Would you and Miss McKinnon care for a cup of tea?'

Marcus smiled. 'Thank you for allowing us to visit so early on a Sunday morning, Caroline. And, yes, a cup of tea would be lovely.'

Caroline scurried out of the room and Marcus turned to the old man in the chair.

'Good morning, Arnold.'

The old man nodded. 'Mornin', My Lord. I've been wondering when you'd turn up at my door.' He motioned for them to sit down on a large chintz sofa, which they did.

Faith and Marcus looked at each other.

'Have you, now?' Marcus said, returning his attention to the old man.

Arnold Grey smiled. 'Ever since I heard the old chapel was going to be used again I've been expecting someone to come and start asking questions.' He turned his attention to Faith. 'You're the lass who's fixing the window, aren't you?'

'Yes,' she said.

The old man nodded again, as if her answer confirmed something. 'You know the sixth Duke made that window for your great-grandmother?'

Marcus leaned forward, clasping his hands together and resting his forearms on his knees. 'That's the story,' he said, 'but until now we haven't been able to verify if it's anything *but* a story. We were hoping that you'd be able to tell us something about Evangeline Huntington.'

At that moment Caroline bustled in with the tea tray, and it took an agonising minute or two before they could resume their conversation. Mr Grey took a sip of his tea and then placed his cup back in its saucer.

'My father told me never to talk of it,' he said. 'But I reckon it's a crying shame what they did to her, and it's about time somebody told the truth.'

Faith's heart began to pound as defiance glittered in the old man's eyes.

'My older sister was her lady's maid,' he explained. 'Terrible upset, she was, when Her Grace left.'

Marcus and Faith shared a glance.

'They were more friends than employer and employee, you see,' Arnold said. 'Evie was a florist's daughter. Sweet as anything, she was, but shy and not very confident. It took a lot for the Duke to convince her to accept him, but he finally wore her down. She thought the world of him, though, and was awful upset when he died so young. But she had the baby to comfort her, and she doted on him.'

Faith reached over and covered Marcus's hand with hers. He'd gone very pale where Mr Grey had been speaking.

'You mean it's all true?' he said quietly. 'My family has been lying all these years?'

The old man didn't say anything, but the sadness in his eyes was confirmation enough.

Faith found it hard to catch her voice. 'So what really happened? Can you tell us?'

He nodded, just once, and then he smiled. 'As soon as I've had my chocolate digestive, I will.'

'That was so sad,' Faith said as they walked back across the park towards the castle.

Marcus reached for her gloved hand and enclosed it in his. He didn't like to think of her being sad, even on someone else's behalf.

She looked off into the distance, shaking her head. 'They were so cruel to treat her like that. So what if she was a florist's daughter? She was the mother of their only heir! That should have counted for something.'

He stopped, placed his hands on her shoulders and turned her to face him. Then he kissed her softly. He could feel the frown on her features, even though he'd closed his eyes, but after a moment her facial muscles relaxed and softened and she kissed him back.

That was better. He liked making Faith feel better.

When they began to walk again she looped her arm through his and he squeezed it closer to his body, keeping it there. 'They did what they thought was right,' he said with a certain amount of resignation. 'They were protecting the family.'

She looked sharply up at him. 'And what about the poor woman they harangued and belittled until she finally cracked and believed what they told her—that her husband had regretted marrying her, that she would only ever be a hindrance to her son and that he'd be better off without her? They practically ran her out of town with a shotgun.'

He sighed. 'It takes a certain kind of strength to survive a family like mine.'

Faith yanked her arm from his and walked ahead. 'I can't believe you're siding with them!' she all but yelled.

He quickened his pace to catch her up, placed a hand on her shoulder. She shrugged it off.

'I didn't mean that I agree with what they did. I just meant that I understand it.'

Head bowed, she looked at him from under her lashes. 'There are no excuses for separating a parent from their child. No excuses at all.'

He nodded, moved his hand to rub her shoulder. 'You're taking this all too personally, Faith. This isn't the same as what happened to you, and it was such a long time ago.'

She shook her head, smiling, but it was all teeth and stretched lips. 'No. You can't consign this to the distant past—not when there's a sad old man sitting by the fire in that castle, aching to know why his mother abandoned him. Because that's what all this is about, isn't it? Duke or no duke, all your grandfather wants to know is that he belongs. Why do you think he stayed away from his home all those years?'

That thought hit Marcus square between the eyes. He jammed his hands in his pockets and picked up speed. 'Is that why *you* stay away from home?'

Her mouth moved and her eyes widened. 'This isn't about me. This is about your family. Don't do what the rest of them do and blame it on the commoner—the outsider.'

He clenched his jaw. That was not what he'd meant and she knew it. He was right, though—about Faith's reluctance to return to the picture-perfect town she painted with such warm words, about her identifying too strongly with his unfortunate great-grandmother.

They walked in silence for a few minutes. Eventually she said, 'Do you want me to come with you when you tell him?'

He looked at her, then shook his head. 'No. This is family business. I think I'd better do this on my own.'

'Fine,' she said, looking anything but. Her mouth drooped and her eyes were large under her woolly hat. 'I'll be where I belong—in the studio, working on the window.'

CHAPTER TEN

MARCUS sat on the sofa, in what he now thought of as Faith's place, and watched his grandfather carefully for a reaction. Bertie had closed his eyes and rested his head against the high back of his winged chair when Marcus had finished talking. Had he done the right thing in being so open about what he and Faith had found? He'd wanted to protect his grandfather from pain, but that hadn't been possible either way.

'Grandfather?' he asked quietly. 'Are you okay?'

Bertie nodded and opened his eyes. 'I don't know if it's better to know that she loved me, that she didn't desert me willingly, or whether I'd prefer to be ignorant still and not be haunted by the idea that, had I started this sooner, I might have met her.' He opened his eyes looked across at Marcus. 'Do you know what happened to her after she left?'

'No, but I have a friend who's a genealogist. He may be able to come up with something. Would that help?'

His grandfather nodded.

Marcus looked into the fire. 'Why couldn't the family have just accepted her? Things were changing—ten years after the Great War ended the world was a different place. It couldn't have mattered so much then.'

His grandfather folded his hands in his lap. 'My uncle Reginald was a small-minded man, petty. He'd always envied my father, I was told, and once he got a chance to have

Hadsborough himself, even by proxy, I'm afraid it rather went to his head.'

Marcus got up and headed over to the window, looked outside at the still-perfect snowscape. 'No wonder you turfed him out on his ear and employed an estate manager when you were old enough.'

He heard rustling behind him, guessed his grandfather was fussing with the papers he kept close to him at all times nowadays.

'What does Faith think about all of this?' he asked.

'She went back to work on Evie's window, as she's now calling it,' Marcus said with a sigh. 'She's taking it all very personally. That's why I came to talk to you on my own.'

'You wouldn't be watching out for her so keenly if you didn't care about her.'

Marcus's insides sank further. He was trying not to care too much, but the boundaries kept getting blurry, and he couldn't always work out if he was on the right side or not any more.

He walked over to the other armchair and sat in it. 'Yes, I do care.'

Though sadness still lingered in his eyes, Marcus's response brought a warmth to Bertie's expression. 'I haven't seen you look at a girl that way since Amanda.'

Marcus expected to flinch at the mention of her name, but it washed over him. He wasn't angry with her any more, he realised. He'd let that go. In fact in the last couple of weeks he'd let a lot of things go. And he couldn't help but think that was Faith's doing. He felt as if he'd come alive since she'd been here—had started to remember who he was before life had taught him to mistrust everything and everyone.

Suddenly Amanda's parting words to him that fateful night made sense. *'I can't do it any more, Marcus,'* she'd said. *'I can't be with this angry, distant man you've become.'*

He'd thought it had just been an excuse—Amanda shifting the blame from herself to him—but now he could see the truth of her words. He'd thought she'd backed off because it wasn't the life they'd pictured together. Titles and castles had been a long way off in the future, then. But he realised now it wasn't Hadsborough and the Huntington name that had sent her running, but him. He'd stopped believing in her, in love. In anything good.

Bertie picked up the photo in a silver frame that was on the table next to his armchair and handed it to Marcus. His grandparents on their wedding day. Bertie looked as if he could burst with pride, and Granny Clara's eyes were shining.

'I knew it the moment I met her,' his grandfather said softly. 'Knew I should grab the chance to have her before she flitted out of my life and some other chap snapped her up. Proposed after one week.'

Marcus nodded. He knew. He'd heard the story a hundred times. He handed the frame back to his grandfather. 'I'm afraid I don't believe in love at first sight.'

He still wasn't sure he believed in love at all. At least he hadn't…

He shook his head. It was foolishness to think that way.

'Love is unreliable,' he said baldly. 'Look at my parents… look at yours!'

His grandfather shrugged, but his eyes were still smiling. 'Of course it's unreliable. Of course you can't pin it down and analyse it. That's what makes it so wonderful. But isn't it worth the risk when it all works out? Your grandmother and I had forty-nine glorious years together.'

Marcus looked into the fire. He knew that, too. He just couldn't quite project into the future and imagine it for himself.

'She came here for a reason, you know.'

Marcus looked up and found his grandfather staring intently at him. He didn't need to ask who he was talking about. 'She came here to fix your bloody window,' he said grimly.

'I know you've had a lot of disappointments in your life,' his grandfather said. 'I know people have let you down again and again. And I know what Harvey did... There have been a lot of shocks to recover from.'

Marcus shook his head, not wanting to hear anything else about his father.

Bertie closed his mouth and thought for a second, then he began to speak again. 'What happened to that adventurous young boy who tried to modify his kite so he could strap himself into it and launch himself off the battlements?'

Marcus blinked. He *had* done that once, hadn't he? Thank goodness the housekeeper had found him and stopped him in time.

Bertie chuckled. 'I know what you're thinking. But wouldn't it have been a marvellous adventure to actually fly?'

He couldn't help smiling. 'You're a delusional old man,' he told his grandfather.

'Maybe,' Bertie said, and then blinked slowly. 'But there's a time for grieving, for licking one's wounds and there's also a time to let yourself heal.' He reached across and patted Marcus's arm. 'The bird with the broken wing is supposed to fly again once it's mended.'

Marcus nodded even as he looked away. That was the problem, wasn't it? What if the wounds went so deep that they never mended? What if the bird tried to fly too soon and came crashing to the ground?

Faith ended the call and put her phone beside her on the table. She picked up her brush and continued working dry cement into the crevasses of the completely re-leaded window panel.

Fabulous timing, Gram.

The emotional blackmail had been hot and hard, but she'd managed to hold her ground. She knew Gram was trying to do what she thought was best for her, but her grandmother didn't understand what it was like. Gram had always been the centre of their little family unit. She'd never been consigned to the fringes as Faith had.

And the bombshell her grandmother had dropped had only made Faith want to stay away all the more.

Her dad—not the biological one, the other one—was back in town. Gram had said he and her mother had been spending a lot of time together. She'd thought that meant fireworks, but Gram had assured her they'd been getting along fine.

One side of her mouth turned down as she thought about that. As much as she wasn't sure she could deal with the Mom and Dad rollercoaster again, the possibility of reconciliation scared her more.

She could imagine it now: Christmas dinner as one big, happy family. Gram, Mom, Greg and her sisters, all laughing and talking and passing the potatoes between each other.

And her.

It had been bad enough thinking about going home anyway. Now she really would be the spare wheel.

She was disgusted with herself for wanting things back the way they had been before Dad had come back on the scene, even if 'normal' for the McKinnon women had meant fractured and dysfunctional. She was a horrible, horrible person.

She glanced up at Basil, who had now been moved into the studio to keep an eye on her. He stared back, offering no sympathy.

Slowly she put her brush down. She couldn't concentrate. She was too wired, waiting for Marcus's knock on the studio door. If it hadn't already been shut she'd have been tempted to slam it in his face when he arrived.

Because that was what he'd done to her—shut her out. Just as she'd started to believe she mattered to him. His words still rang in her head.

Family business...

And she wasn't family, was she? Never would be.

Even so, she was more angry with herself than she was

with him. Why was she surprised? She knew that already. Of course she wasn't family. She'd only been here a few weeks. How on earth had she got to a place where she was upset with him for stating the facts? Somehow she'd got distracted by things like Christmas lights and balls and moonlit mazes, even though she'd tried her hardest not to.

She decided she couldn't stand it any more. She couldn't sit here, meekly waiting for him. They weren't joined at the hip, for goodness' sake. They weren't joined in any way at all. And there'd be plenty of time to finish the window tomorrow.

What she needed was to get some space, some distance, to get her head straight. She didn't owe Marcus Huntington an explanation or a note to say where she was going. She was her own person and she could do what she liked.

She stood up, ignoring Basil's disapproving glare, and put her coat on.

Marcus had searched the entire castle and he couldn't find Faith anywhere. This was definitely a moment when having a sixteen-bedroomed monstrosity for a home was a disadvantage.

He was furious with her for disappearing like a sulky child. He'd known she hadn't liked his decision to go and see his grandfather on his own, but he'd done it for her own good. She would have hated to see Bertie sad like that. The two of them had formed a strong bond in a ridiculously short time.

At least he told himself he was furious. The longer he looked for her, the more his anger chilled into something more anxious. Still, he told himself, he was going to find her and give her a piece of his mind.

This was the third time he'd walked down the corridor that led to the turret bedroom, but this time he noticed something he hadn't picked up on before—the little door that led to the roof was slightly ajar. He stopped and looked at it. As far as he knew Faith didn't even know of its existence. Most people mistook it for a linen cupboard.

He pulled the door open and listened. Nothing. Even so, he found himself climbing the narrow curling stairs, bending his head low to prevent himself from hitting it on the stone above. When he reached the top he pushed an equally tiny door open. Cold air rushed past him. A few more steps and he could see the starlit sky.

At first he didn't see her, but then he spotted a shadow in the corner of the roof, its back to him, arms folded on the battlements, gazing over the lake. He started striding.

She heard him when he was halfway towards her. Even in the dark he saw her stiffen. He opened his mouth—ready to justify himself, ready to explain why he'd had to leave her out of his conversation with his grandfather—but when Faith whirled round and looked at him all those paper defences fluttered away.

He could see it in her eyes—the raw hurt, the disappointment. The pain that *he* had caused. It boomeranged back and hit him square in the chest.

He walked towards her, not saying anything, a bleak expression on his face, and when he reached her he lifted her off her feet, pulled her to him and kissed her as if his life depended on it. Maybe it did. Because all that mattered at this moment was wiping the pain from her eyes, making sure she never, *ever* felt that way again. He couldn't bear it.

She kissed him back, fiercely at first, her latent anger bubbling below the surface. He met her in that place and the heat intensified between them. But with each meeting of their lips they peeled another layer from each other. What had started off as armour clashing against armour slowly became skin exploring skin—and deeper.

When they had finally fought out whatever the hell had been going on between them he dropped one last sweet kiss on her lips, then pulled back and gently brushed one set of glistening lashes with his thumb.

'I didn't mean to upset you,' he said softly, letting his hand fall away.

She caught it and brought it up to her cheek, closed her eyes. 'I understand that now,' she replied, her voice thick. 'It's not that.'

Good. All that needed to be said had been said. Or kissed.

'I don't mean to cry,' she said, shaking her head as more moisture spiked her lashes. 'It's just that sometimes you have a way of making me feel so…so…' She stopped shaking her head, looked right at him. 'Like I'm something precious.'

Her eyes begged him to tell her she wasn't wrong. He placed a hand on either side of her face, stroked the soft skin of her cheeks with the pads of his thumbs. He looked deep into those warm brown eyes and gave her the confirmation she craved.

How, in all her life, had no one ever made Faith McKinnon feel special? Couldn't they see what was right in front of their eyes?

This time he kissed her slowly and tenderly. She seemed to drink it in, as if she couldn't get enough of what he gave her. Marcus knew he'd gladly empty himself of everything he had and everything he was to see her smiling and happy.

He'd done it, hadn't he? Without meaning to, and despite his best efforts not to.

It didn't matter that they hadn't slept together. It didn't matter that he could still picture the hollowness in Amanda's face as she'd walked away from him that last time. He'd leapt off these battlements, not knowing if his wings would hold or not. There was only one thing to do now.

Fly.

Faith's eyes were huge and glistening. Her mouth quivered and crumpled into a wobbly line. Tears spilled over her lashes and she dipped her head, breaking eye contact. He placed his palms either side of her neck and used his thumbs to tip her jaw upwards until she was looking at him again. For a moment he thought she was going to twist her head, or move away, but then she launched herself forward, wrapped her arms around his neck and kissed him back. Kissed him exactly the same way he'd kissed her.

That was when he knew. That was when he discovered his wings worked.

'How…?' she said in a wobbly voice. 'How is it possible? We've only known each other such a short time. Things like this don't happen…not to real people.'

She reached for his upper arm and pinched the skin hard through his sweater.

'Ow!'

She chuckled softly. 'Just checking…'

He smiled back even as he rubbed his arm. 'I thought you were supposed to pinch *yourself* if you thought you were dreaming, not someone else.'

She just kissed him again, laughing as she did so, and crying, too.

When they'd finished she drew in a deep breath, placed a palm on his chest and closed her eyes, as if she was steadying herself.

With a hammering heart, he opened his mouth. 'I don't want this to end yet,' he said. 'Stay with us for Christmas.'

He saw a flicker of something in her eyes before she answered, but he couldn't label it. Fear? Guilt? Doubt?

It didn't really matter, because she wiped all those things away when she pressed her lips against his, kissed him almost desperately, and whispered, 'Yes, I'll stay. I'd love to spend Christmas with you.'

It was dark by the time Marcus unlocked the orangery the following evening. Faith waited as he swung one of the double doors open, then motioned for her to enter in front of him.

She took a couple of steps into the dark and chilly space and he flicked a switch. Uplighters mounted on the pillars between the high windows bathed the vaulted ceiling in a warm glow, blocking out the white pinprick lights beyond the glass.

'*Wow!*' she said, tipping her head back and looking around. 'Impressive.'

'Beautiful, isn't it? There's not much point in keeping it open to the public in the winter, though.'

Low beds, mostly full of bare earth, ran around the perimeter of the vast space. Many of the seasonal plants were dormant, and even the two rows of citrus trees, in large square wooden planters, weren't doing anything interesting.

Faith walked forward and fingered a waxy leaf with her gloved hands.

They'd already looked for lilies everywhere—sculptures in the gardens, books in the library and paintings in the Long Gallery.

'Up this end,' he said, and led the way to a small semi-circular fountain against a wall at the far end. A copper pipe protruded from a marble swan's beak above the pool, and the edges were sculpted to look like wings, meeting in the middle. He shone the beam of his torch into the empty fountain, lighting up a colourful mosaic.

'Lilies!' she said.

Sure enough, against the bright blue background of the mosaic was a stylised pattern of long-stemmed flowers.

She started to hunt round the edge of the fountain. 'There's got to be something here,' she said. 'An inscription or something. There just *has* to be.'

She knelt down on the hard and dusty floor, requested the flashlight he'd brought with him by flapping a hand, and set to work. Uplighters were great mood lighting, but for treasure-hunting they needed a better light source.

After a couple of minutes searching every square millimetre of the fountain—both inside and out—they both stood up again.

'There's nothing there,' she said, brushing a wayward strand of hair out of her eyes and back behind one ear. 'I don't understand it.'

She started roaming, flashlight in hand, looking for anything that might be their clue, and stopped in front of a statue of a young woman, her long hair draped round her naked body as she stared off wistfully into the distance.

Crouching down, she shone the torch at the base of the statue. On the plinth below her feet was a worn inscription.

'I can't make out the first word, but the end bit seems to be numbers.'

Marcus squatted down beside her and she handed him the flashlight. He shone it diagonally across the indentations in the stone, slanting the beam to bring the writing into relief. 'This statue must have been out in the gardens for some years to have received this much wear and tear,' he said. 'But I always remember it being here.'

Faith squinted, trying to make out the shapes. 'It looks like roman numerals,' she said, tracing the three upright lines at the end with the fingers of her free hand.

'I don't know,' he said, shaking his head. 'The third digit isn't evenly spaced like the first two—it's further away.'

She moved her hand to investigate that spot. 'The stone's too worn to tell, but could there have been a colon between the last two digits?'

'Maybe.'

She looked back at him. 'That would make it a reference to *something* Chapter Eleven, Verse One. Can you make out any of that writing at all?'

'I think the first letter is an H,' he said, 'and there's at least another six or seven after that. This might give us enough to go on.' He transferred his gaze to the end of the orangery.

'There's quite a bit of distance between this statue and the fountain. Do you really think they're connected?'

She nodded emphatically. 'They've got to be,' she said seriously. 'They've just got to be.'

His smiled faded, even as his gaze warmed, and then he pulled her to her feet.

For the next couple of minutes they didn't do any clue-hunting of any kind. And Faith didn't care a bit.

When they were together like this she didn't doubt him. However, that didn't stop the old fears shouting high and shrill in her ears when she was on her own. Sometimes she couldn't help turning her head to listen. As much as she hated those voices, they were familiar—and they were wise. They'd saved her from heartache countless times before. But it was a miserable way to live, walled up away from everyone she cared about, never letting anyone close.

She couldn't keep running to her tower and peering at everyone from a distance. It was lonely up there, and cold, and she'd much rather be here, standing in the open door, with Marcus warm in her arms.

Eyes still closed, she kissed him softly, as if she was testing that he was still there—still real—that he hadn't vanished in a puff of smoke.

He kissed her back, pulling her closer, taking her deeper. She went willingly.

This was real. It was.

Now all she had to do was believe it.

CHAPTER ELEVEN

FAITH sat cross-legged on one of the blue sofas in the library, her feet tucked under her knees, a Bible open on her lap, feeling as if she was fizzing inside.

'Well, Hosea, Chapter Eleven, Verse One, doesn't seem right,' she said, making herself concentrate on the tiny print. 'And Habbakkuk doesn't even have that many chapters, so I'm flipping over to the New Testament to see what the only other H book says…' She parted the book nearer the book and began thumbing through the thin pages. 'Ah…Hebrews, Eleven-One…'

Marcus came and sat down beside her. 'What does it say?'

She read it in silence. All the fizzing stopped.

Then she read it again, just to make sure, before saying the words out loud. '"Now faith is the substance of things hoped for, the evidence of things not seen."' She slapped the book closed and dumped it on the sofa. 'Great.'

Marcus leaned over her, picked up the Bible and had a look for himself.

Faith waited while he read. 'There's only one Faith I can think of on this estate—apart from me, of course.'

Marcus closed the book and rested in it his lap, his finger still marking the place. 'The window…'

Yes, the window.

'It's a dead end, isn't it?' she said, finding her voice suddenly hoarse. 'Your great-grandfather never finished laying out his clues, or they were never there in the first place. We've just been stringing together bits of evidence that were never really connected. It's all been for nothing.'

She stood up. She needed to go somewhere—for a walk, preferably—but it was dark and freezing cold. The only option was to retreat to her turret.

Marcus got to his feet. 'Not for nothing, Faith… We found out the truth about Bertie's mother. You gave him that.'

'Yes, and what good has that done?'

She'd hoped Bertie would be happier, but he'd been very quiet and withdrawn since Marcus had spoken to him. She walked to the window and folded her arms, staring out at the black lake, only distinguishable from the dark lawns by the play of a half-hidden moon on its surface. The fragments of light reached for each other, trying to assemble themselves into a whole, but the wind on the water kept ripping them apart.

She looked back at Marcus, scowling at her from the fireplace, looking impossibly handsome.

She'd fallen in love with him, hadn't she? She'd done everything she'd promised herself she wouldn't and let herself believe in the fairytale.

Okay, no. She hadn't exactly let herself believe, but she'd stopped herself from *not* believing—which was just as dangerous. She'd invested in it all oh-so-much-more than she'd meant to. Just like the non-existent treasure hunt.

'That clue on the statue was probably nothing of the sort. We were just jumping to conclusions, seeing what we wanted to see.'

As she stood at the glass, staring out into the blackness, she realised she probably wasn't the first woman to look out of this window and feel this way.

'I wonder if Evie stood here,' she said softly as Marcus came to stand behind her. 'Mr Grey said she used to stare out of the castle windows crying after your great-grandfather died.'

He suddenly gripped her shoulders. 'Of *course*,' he said quietly.

She shrugged his hands off and turned to face him. 'What?'

'Something Arnold Grey said the other day that I dismissed as an odd comment suddenly makes sense. I didn't understand at the time.'

Her forehead creased. 'What was it?'

'Do you remember? He said his sister told him she didn't just stand and stare out of any particular window. She looked out of *all* of them in turn. I think Great Uncle Reginald told her about his brother's letter—about the message.'

Her heart lightened. 'You think she found it? That there really was one? Do you think she worked out what it all meant?'

He shook his head. 'I think the old—' He stopped, didn't say the word she guessed he wanted to. 'I think that dear old Great-Uncle Reggie gave her the message, but didn't elaborate. The work in the chapel was supposed to be a surprise. And why would my great-grandmother have cried so much if she'd found the comfort such a message should have brought?'

Faith's face fell. 'Oh. How cruel.' She shook her head. 'She knew the message was in a window, but they didn't tell her *which* window, and she spent years looking before she gave up and accepted the lies they fed her.'

His expression grew hard. 'Even so,' he said, his voice stony, just like on the first morning she'd met him, 'she shouldn't have given up.'

Faith turned back to the window, placed her hands on the cold glass. 'Not everyone is like you Huntingtons, you know. Some of us have blood flowing through our veins, not steel.'

'What's that supposed to mean?'

She watched his reflection in the darkened window. 'Just that you're a special breed. Not everyone is as strong as that.

Sometimes people have to know when it's time to give up and walk away.'

He was looking at her, his gaze intense. She refused to turn around.

'But think of the trail her husband was preparing for her—it was proof of some kind, a memory she could have taken forward with her. If not for herself, then she should have stuck it out for her son.'

Faith threw her hand in the air, exasperated. 'There *was* no trail! It was all in our minds. All it did was lead us right back to square one. And even if there was, Evie never knew about it!'

'Then why did someone change the window? It had to have meant something.'

She shook her head. 'They just made the same mistake we did. Thought it meant something when it didn't. They just decided not to take any chances and hide it anyway, even if they didn't understand what it meant.'

His face was hard, like the stone wall behind him. 'How can you be married to someone for five years and not believe they loved you?'

Faith glared back at him. Pretty much the same way you could believe your father adored you when he wasn't even genetically connected to you, when the overriding feeling he had when he looked at you was pain and humiliation. People could believe in the stupidest things if they wanted to badly enough.

She shook her head. 'You don't know. You don't understand what it's like to want to fit in somewhere so bad, but to know deep down that it's never going to happen. To know that one day you'll just be on your own again.'

Tears started to flow down her face and she swiped them away angrily. She sucked in a breath, trapped that quivering feeling in her lungs.

His expression softened and he moved towards her.

'Faith…I don't want to fight with you. The truth is that we may never know exactly what happened.'

He reached her, folded his arms around her and held her close. She burrowed her face into his chest and stayed there. She knew she should breathe out, release this shaky, quivery feeling inside and let her muscles relax, but she couldn't seem to work out how.

'Has your genealogist friend come up with anything?' she asked, pulling away a little and brushing the hair from her face. She needed to talk about something different before she completely fell apart.

'He left a message on my voicemail earlier,' Marcus replied. 'I'm going to call him in the morning.'

She nodded. In the morning her reason for being here would be at an end. No more window to fix, no more phantom trail to follow.

'You're right. Of course you're right. It's dumb to fight about this.' She pulled herself away from him and smiled, hid behind that outward show of happiness. 'I…I need a bath, I think.' She stepped out of his embrace. 'I'll see you at dinner.'

And then she ran, along corridors and up the winding stairs, higher and higher, until she reached her turret and shut the door behind her. She ran into the *en suite* bathroom, wrenched the taps so the bath flooded with scalding water, and stripped off all her clothes. While the water gurgled and the steam rose she covered her face with her hands and wept.

This was ridiculous. She felt… She felt… As if someone had died. As if she'd lost something precious. And all she'd done was race around for the past few weeks on a fool's errand, chasing a dream that wasn't really there.

She lay in the hot water and churned it all over in her mind. She couldn't imagine Evie as a coward, that she'd run for nothing. A mother would never leave her child like that unless she was pushed to the limit.

Poor Evie. Faith knew what that was like—to wake up

one day and realise you were a stranger in your own home, to discover the family you'd trusted had lied to you your whole life. Evie had trusted happy-ever-after and it had let her down badly. She'd believed. She'd really believed. And it hadn't been enough.

That thought had Faith springing from the tub and into her bedroom, panic rising in her chest. She closed her eyes. She loved Marcus. She knew she did. And everything inside her told her loved her, too. Yet...

She held her breath, tried to push the shaky feeling down with the air she was holding in her mouth and throat.

Marcus was her fairytale.

She wanted him so, so much. But that didn't mean the last page wouldn't close. Didn't mean the story wouldn't end the way it always did—with the words *The End.*

Faith yanked open the dresser, looking for her underwear. It sat there, plain and functional, in the ornate, perfumed walnut drawer. She looked at it for a second, then pulled all of her panties and bras out, not caring when the elastic on one item got caught somewhere and she had to wrench it free. And then she stuffed them into the front pocket of her case and zipped it up tight.

The next morning Marcus went to find Faith, only to discover she was already on her way to the chapel to put the repaired bottom section back in the window. She hadn't come down for dinner the night before, and when he'd knocked softly on her door there had been no answer. He was worried about her.

He also felt guilty. He should have realised she hadn't been in any shape to see straight about that blasted last clue.

He arrived at the chapel to find her already at work, quiet and composed. He breathed out a little and instead of disturbing her sat in one of the back pews and silently watched her. Although she didn't turn round, he sensed she knew he was there.

When all was finished she stood back, hands on hips.

He stood up and walked towards her. 'It looks wonderful,' he said.

Pity that the sky was dark and threatening rain, dulling the impact of the bright, jewel-coloured glass.

She turned and smiled, but it lacked its normal lustre. 'All done. My work here is over.'

He closed the distance between them. 'Wait until you see your window in all its glory at the Carol Service.'

She glanced over her shoulder at the window. 'It's not my window—it's not even Evie's. It's just a pretty picture made out of glass that a rich man paid for.'

Ouch. Okay. She was obviously still smarting from the whole dead end thing. He decided to tell her his news, the information that would let her know their search for Evie's treasure trail had at least turned up something good. Hopefully that would allow her to get a little perspective on the matter.

'We've located a relation of Bertie's in the East End of London.'

'Really?'

He nodded. 'My friend discovered that Evie remarried five years after she left Hadsborough, had another child. Her daughter's daughter is still alive. Bertie has a niece.' He smiled. 'You won't believe it, but she's a florist—carrying on the family tradition.'

'What does Bertie think about all of this?'

Marcus frowned. 'Surprisingly, he's a little bit cool about the idea of meeting her. But I'm going to her invite her down for the Carol Service. He'll feel differently when he sees her.'

Faith's expression darkened. 'Why don't you *listen* to your grandfather? If he doesn't want to meet her, he doesn't want to meet her.'

But now was the perfect time. He didn't want his grandfather to be engulfed by the sadness that had been creeping over him. This time he wasn't going to stand idly by while someone he loved sank further and further, stupidly trusting it would all work itself out in the end.

'I know it will help him,' he said.

She shook her head and picked up her bag.

He took a deep breath. 'A genealogist could help you find your father, too.'

Faith went still. 'Don't push, I said, Marcus. That's my business, not yours.'

A horrible feeling settled in his stomach. This was not going well. And he had no idea why. He decided to try another approach.

He reached out, caught Faith's hand. She looked down, and then back up at him. He leaned in and pressed a soft kiss on her lips—a kiss that was supposed to have been a prelude to more. But he pulled back, frowning. Her lips felt cold and she'd barely responded.

'What's wrong?' he asked.

She shook her head, her eyes blank. 'Nothing.'

'I'll butt out,' he said. 'If you don't want to find your father, that's totally up to you.'

She nodded. On the surface she looked pleased. But everything about her seemed weighed down. Grey...

'Okay. Thank you.'

That was when he realised what was wrong. This was the wrong Faith. This was black and white Faith. Where was the warm, vibrant, caring woman he'd been kissing last night? He knew she'd been upset about the window, the treasure trail... He just hadn't realised how much it had rocked her, how heavily she'd invested in it.

'It's more than that, isn't it?' he said.

He and Faith had never lied to each other before. They might have hidden behind their respective walls, but they'd always, *always* been straight with each other.

She looked away and wrapped her arms around her middle. 'I can't stay for Christmas after all, Marcus. I need to go home, to see my family.' She turned and looked him in the eye. 'I'm sorry.'

That was when he realised for the first time in weeks he had no idea what was going on in her head. And he'd seen that look on a woman's face before. Emotionally checked out. That was what it was. He didn't like that at all.

'Then I'll come with you,' he said.

A horrible idea was forming in his head—one that told him if he let her go now she'd never come back.

She hugged herself tighter, moved her weight onto her heels, as if she was going to back away from him. 'I need to do this on my own,' she said, her voice quiet. 'You more than anyone know that I have some issues to sort out back there.'

He nodded. He didn't like it, but he understood it.

'What date are you back?' he asked, testing. 'I'll come and meet you at the airport.'

This time she did step back. 'Not sure. I might have to go straight up to York.' She shrugged one shoulder. 'I'll call you.'

Now she hadn't just blocked him out, she was lying to him. He had two choices—get scared or get angry. He chose the latter.

He stepped towards her. 'Tell me what's going on,' he demanded, knowing his tone had more of a growl than he'd intended it to. Unfortunately it was the tone guaranteed to make Faith McKinnon dig her heels in harder.

That was when she let him have the truth. With both barrels.

Her chin lifted. 'I'm going to the cottage for a few days. I need time to think.'

The rage started to bubble out of control inside him. More lies. He'd been right to get worried. Faith McKinnon was putting on her running shoes.

'You're not her—you're not Evie,' he said, in a low tone full of warning. 'Don't take the coward's way out. All I'm asking is that you trust we have something we can start to build on.'

'Are you calling me a coward?'

'No.' *Yes.*

'Then what are you saying?'

He shook his head, and when he spoke his jaw was tight. He had to force the words out. 'That running away won't solve anything. It doesn't avoid the mess. It just leaves it for someone else to clear up—I think my great-grandmother demonstrated that admirably. Bertie is living proof of her mistake.'

'I'm not running away,' she said, folding her arms again, tighter this time. 'I'm going home. There's a difference.'

Well, if there was one he couldn't see it. And she was slipping away. If he didn't do something drastic in the next few moments she'd always be out of his reach.

'But I love you!'

That definitely hadn't been the tone he'd intended to use the first time he told her that, but he was good and fired up now, and he hadn't been able to help it.

She flinched at the words—actually flinched. That wasn't good.

'It's not enough, is it? I'm not sure anything I offered would be good enough for you. What would be enough to make you stay, Faith?' He really was shouting now. 'And what happens if you never find it? What legacy will you leave behind for your children? If you ever let a man close enough to have any... What is all this running going to teach them about life?'

She walked backwards, shaking her head. 'Don't you pin that on me. You don't know anything about what my life has been like.'

'Faith!' He grabbed for her, but she kept backing away. 'I'm just trying to protect you from making a mistake you're going to regret.'

'The only thing I need protection from right at this moment,' she said coldly, 'is you. And if I am making a mistake then it's mine to make.'

He'd tried to keep the caveman part of himself from taking over, to give the Earl a chance to sort this out in a reasonable manner, but now the Earl had failed the caveman pushed himself to the front and took charge. Marcus stepped forward, crushed Faith to him and kissed her stiff resolve away. He kissed her until she was breathless and panting and malleable in his hands. He would *make* her see sense.

She stepped back, wrapped her arms around her middle again and looked at him, eyes wide, chest rising and falling. 'That doesn't change anything,' she said, quietly and far too reasonably. And then she walked away.

Just like Evie. But she could do it if she wanted to. She *could* stay. His great-grandmother had just lacked the gumption.

But Marcus believed in Faith, believed she was strong enough. Why wouldn't she?

He marched right up to the window and considered putting his fist through all those pretty bits of glass to see them splinter and dance.

He'd been so stupid. After all his warnings to himself he'd been seduced by that feeling of destiny, of being soul mates—yes, even blasted love at first sight! And he'd fallen right back down into that deep pit he'd only just managed to haul himself out of. He'd let himself believe that Faith McKinnon was the woman he'd been waiting for—the woman who would stand by his side, face thick or thin with him.

But she wasn't. She really wasn't.

It made him so angry to see her giving up on herself, giving up on *them,* when he knew she was capable of more.

He followed her and stepped in front of her, making her look at him. 'Then I think it's a good idea that you go,' he said, his voice low and his teeth clenched. 'Because I need a woman who can think beyond her own selfish need for self-protection and who can *give* herself. I want a partner, not a reluctant conscript. And until that changes, you're right—you don't belong here with me.'

Faith's mouth moved and a small croaking sound came out, then she spun around and ran from the chapel, her coat flapping in her self-made breeze.

Faith dragged her last case all the way from the castle to the visitor car park and stuffed it into the trunk of her car. With every lopsided step she could feel him watching her from any one of a hundred mullioned windows, but when she turned round he was never there. When the trunk was closed and her purse was sitting on the passenger seat she pulled the keys from her pocket. They dangled in her hand.

She had one last thing to do before she left Hadsborough. One last goodbye to say.

She took the long route back to the little chapel, avoiding going close to the castle. As she half jogged she kept glancing at the greying sky. There was a tiny patch of blue off in the distance, but she didn't hold out much hope. It looked as if she'd be driving to Whitstable in the rain.

The chapel looked beautiful—finally ready for the Carol Service. Tall wrought-iron stands held thick cream candles, and holly and ivy dripped from the ends of the compact pews, tied in red ribbons. She ignored all of that and headed for the little side window—the one that had started it all.

She hadn't been able to take a proper look earlier. Not while Marcus had been pushing her and criticising her.

A flash of sadness shot through her. She wanted so badly to believe it could all come true, that she could find her happy ending here with him. But this was real life, and real life dealt in disappointment and compromise.

He'd said he loved her.

But he'd also said she wasn't worthy of him, and he was right. She was running. The only reason she'd decided to go home for Christmas was because it was less scary than trying to stay here and work it out with Marcus.

She let out a hollow laugh. Finally she'd run so far and so

long the only place she had to go back to was home. There was a sense of ironic justice in that, she guessed. But run she would. Because she didn't think she could stay here with that familiar creeping feeling that something was out of place still dogging her. Especially when that 'something' usually turned out to be her.

She shook her head. *Save the pity party for later, Faith. When you've got a glass of wine and a hot bath to console you.* She was here to look at the window, not to pick over the ruins of a dream she never should have let take root.

So she looked at the window. It really was beautiful. As she stared at the dull picture suddenly a beam of sunlight hit the outside of the glass. Faith gasped. At once the colours became bright and saturated, almost living.

The window was nothing without light. She stood there, motionless, until the wind pushed the clouds on further and everything fell dark again.

'Thank you,' she whispered to whoever was listening. At least she had that to take away with her.

CHAPTER TWELVE

FAITH sat on the end of the double bed in the ten-feet-by-ten-feet bedroom of the tiny cottage on Whitstable's seafront, staring out of the window at an angry sea. Ironically, the whole cottage had been decorated in 'New England' style, with white and blue painted wood and deep red and navy chequered pillows and curtains everywhere.

Still staring at the waves as they crashed over the beach, ripping the pebbles backwards and then hurling them onto the shore again, she reached for her cellphone and punched in the only speed dial number, then waited for the person at the other end to pick up.

'Hi, Gram.'

She heard a gasp of surprise and delight on the other end of the line. 'Hey, honey. Good to hear your voice again.'

She fidgeted and smoothed the comforter underneath her rear end. 'I'm coming home, Gram. It was only the window job that was holding me up and...well, I've finished that now.'

'Oh, Faith! That's wonderful!'

She knew she'd feel like an outsider back in Beckett's Run, but at least she knew how to handle it there; she'd been dealing with it most of her adult life.

She took a breath and revved up to ask the question she'd been dreading to ask since their last chat. 'Will Greg...Dad... definitely be coming to Christmas dinner?'

'Yes, sweetie. He's really looking forward to seeing you.'

'Oh…good,' she replied, aware she sounded less than enthused.

Gram took a breath, and Faith knew some of her grandmother's home truths were on their way. They were as famous as her chocolate cookies with powdered sugar, but being on the receiving end of them was nowhere near as pleasant.

'I know you've found it tough with him,' Gram said, and the warmth in her tone made Faith want to cry. 'It almost killed him when he found out he wasn't your biological father. I know he didn't handle it very well at first.'

You think? she was tempted to say. When an eight-year-old can tell you don't want to look at her, you're not handling it very well.

'But it was only because he loved you so much,' Gram continued. 'He did the best he could. And when he got to grips with it he really tried, but he said you were always so distant, locked away inside yourself. Many years later he told me he wondered if you'd found out, and that you didn't want him to be your dad any more.'

Tears slid down Faith's cheeks. She'd have given anything to have felt the same confidence and comfortableness with him that Hope and Grace seemed to have. She hadn't realised he'd felt it, too, though—the distance. And if what Gram had said was right, maybe the gulf between them all these years hadn't been just his doing.

Her grandmother must have sensed she was having trouble choking a word or two out, because she abruptly changed the subject. 'How's Bertie?'

Faith found herself smiling through her tears. She reached for a tissue from the box on the nightstand and dried her eyes. 'He's an old charmer—but I guess you knew that about him already.'

Gram let out a chuckle that verged on the girlish. 'Yes, I did once. It's nice to know he hasn't changed.'

Faith screwed the tissue up and aimed it at the bin near the dressing table. She missed. 'I got the impression he was in love with you once.' She got up, retrieved the wad of tissue from the floor and dropped it in its rightful home. 'If he'd asked you to marry him would you have said yes?'

'Oh, he did ask,' Gram said, sounding for all the world as if he'd merely asked her to go down to the store for a quart of milk. 'I turned him down.'

Faith's mouth hung open. She'd always assumed that Bertie hadn't asked because Gram wouldn't have been 'suitable'.

'Why?' she said, so quietly it was almost a whisper. 'Because you knew it wouldn't work? That you wouldn't fit into his life?'

Gram sighed. 'Because he was a wandering soul, honey. He was always restless, and I knew that was never going to change. I wanted roots and a family and a home—that's why it wouldn't have worked. Not because of who we were or where we came from.'

'But that *would* have been a problem if you'd wanted to, right?'

'Maybe. I don't know.' Another sigh. 'I worry about the same thing for you.'

Faith swallowed. Gram was the most sensible person she knew, and if Gram could see problems with a romance between a girl from small-town Connecticut and a man who would be a duke one day she was probably right.

'It's okay,' she said. 'I'm not thinking about marrying the grandson.'

Not any more.

Gram chuckled. 'I'd be delighted if I thought some nice young man was going to propose, but I meant that you remind me of Bertie in other ways—you've got those same restless feet.'

Faith frowned. That was nonsense, as Bertie would say.

All she'd ever wanted was to find somewhere she could unpack for good and finally belong.

'Well, just be glad those restless feet are bringing me home for the holidays,' she said, with more levity than she felt.

'I am, honey. I am.' There was that tone again, warm like maple syrup. Faith reached for another tissue from the box, just in case.

'Listen,' Gram said, 'this call must be costing you a fortune. Let's save the rest of the catching up for when we're face to face.'

'Sure.' Faith breathed in deep. 'Love you, Gram.'

'Love you, too, honey.'

And then she was gone. Faith discovered her reach for the tissues had been somewhat prophetic.

The front door to the little white cottage was painted a summery sky-blue. It seemed artificially bright in this pretty but deserted off-season seaside town only a few days before Christmas. Marcus bunched his fist and rapped on the matt paint. He and Faith McKinnon had unfinished business, and he wasn't letting her run away until they faced it.

A few moments later he heard footsteps in the hallway, and then the door cracked open. By the look on Faith's face she was considering slamming it closed again. He opened out his hand and applied gentle pressure to the wood.

'We need to talk before you go,' he said.

Indecision swirled in her eyes.

He didn't push the door. 'And I've got something for you—a Christmas present,' he added, lifting up the large paper bag that was weighing down his left arm.

She nodded and let the door swing open, but she retreated down the hallway and into a small living room before he got too close. He followed, leaving his left arm behind him so not to bang the bag on the walls of the narrow passageway.

She stood by the window of the tiny living room and folded

her arms. He stayed by the door and gently lowered the bag to the floor. He cleared his throat. 'There were things we both said that we shouldn't have, and things we probably didn't say that we should.'

She nodded again. It didn't mean she'd dropped those mile-high barriers an inch, though.

'I was angry,' he said, 'because I think we have something unique, and I don't want us to throw it away without giving it a chance.'

Her arms squeezed tighter around her midriff. 'I am giving it a chance.'

He took a shallow breath. No, she wasn't. She wasn't going to let her drawbridge down an inch, was she? Well, he might as well carry on saying what he'd come here to say.

'I want you to know that I heard what you said—about you and about Bertie. No more pushing.'

A faint smile flickered at the corners of her lips. 'You can't help it, Marcus. But the way you look out for those you care about is what I lo—' She broke off and looked away. 'What I admire most about you. Don't change on my account.'

'I have changed. But *because* of you, not for you.'

And then, because she didn't respond, and because there was no point in having a one-sided conversation with a brick wall, he picked up the paper bag and offered it to her. 'Merry Christmas.'

She frowned slightly, but she accepted it from him. The present inside wasn't gift-wrapped, so she spotted what it was as soon as she looked down. Her mouth fell open.

'You're giving me Basil?'

Yep. It had been staring at him when he'd gone back to Faith's empty studio. He'd decided it needed a good home.

She put the bag down and carefully lifted the creature out, now with a big red bow tied round his neck, and placed him on the sofa. Basil stared warily at his new surroundings with his orange glass eyes. Marcus decided that if he'd been able to talk he'd have probably asked to go back inside his filing cabinet.

Faith shrugged, her hands flapping as she searched for something to say.

'Nothing says *I love you* like a stuffed badger,' she finally managed, and he saw her regret at her choice of words even before she uttered the last syllable.

'Quite.'

She raised a hand to her eyes and rubbed them. 'Don't make me cry, Marcus. I've done enough of that already.'

'Then don't cry,' he said softly, stepping towards her and holding out his hand. 'Say goodbye.'

Goodbye. It sounded so final. And she knew it, too. She didn't say anything about *au revoir,* or it being just for now. At least she'd stopped lying to him.

She looked at his open palm with a similar expression to the badger's, but she eventually relented and slid her smaller, paler hand into his.

There it was again. That feeling. The sense that something deep in the core of him resonated with her. She blinked but didn't look away. Neither of them moved.

Marcus realised he didn't want to let go, didn't want to spend the rest of his life wondering if he'd ever find this again with someone else. But after a few breathless moments he released her fingers. He wasn't going to chase her if she ran.

He prepared himself for what he'd really come to say— properly this time.

'I love you,' he said, and waited for a response.

He thought it would feel as if his skin was being flayed off, to hear those words come out of his mouth and receive no echo, but instead a weight lifted from him. It was liberating.

Her eyes filled with tears and her lip wobbled. And then she did say it back. Not with her mouth, but with her eyes, still refusing to pull down those walls.

He lifted his chin. 'I said you didn't know how to give yourself. I was wrong.'

He saw it in her face, the moment she relived the other things he'd shouted after her.

You don't belong...

He stepped forward and saw the panic in her eyes. The pure fear. It confirmed his worst suspicions.

'That wasn't true either,' he added, picking up on her silent communication. 'I think you belong at Hadsborough with me, but...' He paused, prepared himself to deliver the truth he could no longer protect her from. 'But until you *let* yourself belong somewhere you never will. And no amount of chasing after you will change that,' he said. 'So if you want to go...go. I'm not going to stop you.'

He clenched his jaw. Even though he understood it, it still made him angry. She was wasting so much.

'I want to,' she said, her voice wavering. 'I really do.'

There was such pain in her eyes that he truly believed her, and seeing it there made him want to pull her to him and wrap his arms around her. Instead he clenched his fists and held them rigid by his sides. It was either that or start yelling again, which probably would make her bolt all the faster. He'd promised himself he'd end it properly this time—leave with some dignity, not behave like some raving Neanderthal.

Even if she tried she'd fail. Because until she was truly ready she'd always end up running out on him. And that would just set the cycle of rejection spinning again. Faith McKinnon was the only one who could stop it, and he had to accept that she didn't know how. Not yet.

He couldn't resist one last parting shot, though.

'I've one last thing to say. You were right—Evie didn't know the truth when she ran from Hadsborough. But *you* know. Deep down, you know. And you're still running.'

And then he was walking back down the hall and out of the cottage. As he passed the window he glanced in and saw

Faith standing there, the moth-eaten badger clutched to her chest, plinth and all, with tears streaming down her face.

Basil was now sitting on top of the bookcase in the tiny cottage's living room. Faith spent most of that evening staring at him and sipping red wine. The television remained unplugged and her paperback book remained unopened. The badger stared back at her, no help at all.

She turned the events of the past few weeks over and over in her mind—much in the way the endless surf captured and rolled the pebbles on the shore outside her window. She thought about another window, about the stupid romantic trail that never was, and about Evangeline Groggins—her maiden name—florist's daughter and runaway mother.

Had Evie been a coward?

Was *she*?

Had she identified too strongly with Bertie's mother, as Marcus had suggested? It had been so easy to understand why she had left, how she must have had her fill of trying to fit in, always feeling out of place, always feeling like an unwanted reminder. Who wouldn't crumble under that sort of pressure?

Marcus, she thought, as she took another long sip of her wine. Marcus wouldn't crumble. He wouldn't give up. He just wasn't made that way.

But she was. She was a coward. Too scared to stay and fight for the man she loved. Even when he'd given her a second chance she'd just stood there, frozen to the spot, too much of a jellyfish to think, let alone speak.

But Evie hadn't got off lightly. She'd paid a high price for her freedom. Bertie had, too. Marcus had been right about that as well, damn him. And she suspected he'd hit the nail on the head when he'd told her running away didn't solve anything—that you just left others to foot the bill for you. Had she done that to her family? Had she hurt them in ways she hadn't even realised?

She thought of Gram, of her sweet lilac letters and how she ached for her girls to come home...

Yes. The Earl had been right about that, too.

And about what Gram had said about her being a wandering soul? Well, she could see now that she had taken as much as she could from her family, and then had just...checked out. For so long she'd tried to play peacemaker, felt the responsibility for keeping them all together, but once she'd found out the truth she'd shut down, and she'd never really woken up again.

She put her wine glass down. 'Oh, Basil,' she said, standing up and moving over to place a hand on his rough, patchy fur. 'I've been such a fool.'

How could anyone get close if she was keeping them at arm's length? And how could they include her if she walled herself up in her own little tower like Rapunzel and refused to come down?

She'd made herself an outsider, hadn't she?

She grabbed the wine bottle and sloshed some more Merlot into her glass, because the thoughts that followed really had her shaking.

There was only so much time a woman and a badger could spend cooped up together in a tiny little fake New England cottage without one of them going stark staring mad. Faith suspected the badger might be doing the better job of staying sane and so, despite the driving wind that lifted her hair by its roots and made it dance, she ventured out into the cold winter morning.

It was a Sunday, but plenty of cute little coffee shops and art galleries and nice little boutiques were open. She didn't stop at any of them, but when she passed a little florist's shop she paused at the window. It wasn't even a trendy one, with big bouquets in bulbs of cellophane keeping the flowers hydrated. It was the sort of shop you'd go to get your elderly aunt a pot plant, but a little white ceramic planter in the window drew her attention.

She stared at it for a second, then stepped inside the shop and looked around. 'Excuse me,' she said to the woman behind the counter. 'What is that plant in the window? The little shrub with the yellow flowers.'

The woman looked skyward for a second. *'Hypericum calycinum,'* she said, with the air of a woman who knew what she was talking about. 'One of the plants also known as the Rose of Sharon. Pretty, isn't it? Make a nice Christmas present,' she added hopefully.

'I'll take it,' Faith said, surprising herself. There was no way she could take it home on the plane—especially as she already had an unwieldy badger-shaped bit of hand luggage to deal with.

The woman fetched the plant. 'A hundred years ago someone who planted this in their garden would have known what it meant,' she said as she put it in a thin blue-and-white-striped carrier bag.

Faith got the idea the shop had been quiet for days and its owner was in desperate need of someone to chat to. 'What *does* it mean?' she asked almost absently as she rummaged for some cash.

'Love never fails,' the woman said, sighing. 'It's sad no one understands the language of flowers any more... Some of these *avant-garde* things that florist up the high street does! She has no idea of all the horrible things she's wishing her customers.'

Faith stood open-mouthed, staring at the plastic bag. She felt as if she'd been slapped upside the head with her grandmother's iron skillet.

A florist.

Evie Groggins had been a *florist's* daughter!

* * *

Once again a stranger was sitting nervously in the corner of the sofa in the yellow drawing room. The middle-aged woman was squeezing her handbag ever so tightly, Marcus thought. She looked as if she might jump like a frightened rabbit if either he or his grandfather even breathed hard.

'It's very kind of you to come, Donna,' Bertie said, smiling as he stirred his cup of tea.

Donna nodded, but her eyes were wide. 'I can't get over it,' she mumbled. 'The likes of you and me being related… I always knew Granny was a bit of a lady, but…' She shook her head again. 'I can't get over it,' she repeated faintly.

'And you're a florist?' Marcus asked, trying to draw her out, to make her feel more comfortable.

'That's right. Third generation. I run the shop that Granny and Grandpa started before the war—' She looked nervously at Bertie, then back at Marcus. 'Sorry… I didn't mean to mention him.' She squeezed the handbag harder.

'That's quite all right, my dear,' his grandfather said. 'I'm just glad to know a little bit about what happened to her.'

Donna looked up and smiled. 'She was a nice lady. Gentle…quiet… She had a lovely way about her—like you do, if you don't mind me saying, sir.'

'Was she happy?' his grandfather said, doing a good job of hiding his pain behind his smile.

'I think so.' Donna looked across at Marcus. 'At least she didn't seem *un*happy.' She stopped abruptly, as if a thought had just popped into her head. 'Except at Christmas,' she said, smiling faintly. 'Which is odd, isn't it? Because that's normally a happy time.'

'How so?'

She pulled a face. 'It's nothing, really. Something silly… It's just that every Christmas morning, when everyone was laughing and shouting and opening presents, she'd put on her hat and coat and go for a walk—no matter what the weather. She'd be gone for a few hours and then she'd come back again, smile, say she was ready now and then she'd cook the Christmas dinner. Did it every year like clockwork.'

Bertie's tea cup rattled on its saucer and Marcus raced forward to take it out of his hand.

'Oh, dear!' Donna said, standing up so quickly she almost knocked her own cup over. 'I haven't said something out of turn, have I?'

Bertie shook his head. 'No, my dear. Quite the opposite, in fact.'

Marcus picked up Donna's tea, handed it to her and motioned for her to sit down again. 'Christmas Day was my grandfather's birthday, you see...'

'Anyway,' Bertie said, and placed his hands on the arms of his chair to push himself to standing, 'no matter, my dear. Now...let's go and take a look at this window that started all the fuss...'

All three of them were standing in front of the window, admiring it, when there was a crash at the other end of the chapel. Marcus turned to see something come flying through the door.

It took him a second to realise that something was Faith.

She waved a couple of crumpled sheets of paper at them as she kept running towards them. They looked like something that had been printed out from the internet and then chewed up and spat out by a dog.

'The window! It's been there all along!' she said breathlessly. 'The message has been there all along—right under our noses!' She was standing in front of them now, and she paused to rest her hands on her knees, hunched over, and dragged in some much-needed oxygen. 'Flowers...' she said weakly. 'The language of flowers...'

Donna turned to look at the stained glass again. 'Oh, yes! I can see what you mean! There's ivy and daisies, lemon blossom and lavender...even roses...'

Faith stood up so fast Marcus guessed she was seeing stars. 'You mean you know about this stuff?'

Bertie, who was looking far from displeased at Faith's sudden and unscheduled interruption, smiled at her. 'Faith, I'd like to introduce you to my niece—well, my half-niece—Donna.'

Faith's eyes grew wide. She reached forward and shook the other woman's hand. 'Lovely to meet you.' She waved the sheets of paper again. 'There was only so much I could find on the web, and I wasn't sure what some of them were…'

Donna was touching some of the flowers lower down on the window, frowning.

'Do you know what they all mean?' Faith asked. 'Would the words fit together to form a sentence or a phrase?'

The other woman smiled softly at her. 'Much simpler than that. Some of these flowers represent the same things.' She looked at Bertie. 'Did you say your father made this for Granny?'

His grandfather nodded.

Donna's smiled warmed further. 'She would have liked this if she'd seen it.'

'What does it all mean?' Bertie asked.

Donna turned back to the window. 'Well, the roses symbolise love, with each colour and type meaning something slightly different. The daisies and lemon blossom mean fidelity and loyal love, and the others…they all have meanings to do with ardent devotion and marriage. Oh, how odd…' Donna tipped her head on one side. 'That woman in the middle of them…she looks like photos of Granny when she was younger.'

That made the other three stop and stare at the window again.

Faith couldn't stop looking at Marcus all the way through high tea, while Donna and Bertie chatted away like old friends in the background. It wasn't that he looked any different, just that she felt different—just like the window. Now she was looking at him in the right way she could suddenly see all the things she'd been blind to.

She desperately wanted to find some time to be alone with him, to tell him Rapunzel had finally hired a bulldozer and done some much-needed demolition work. But after tea it was time for the Carol Service, and everybody wanted to talk to Bertie and Marcus about the chapel, about how perfect it looked and how excited they were it was going to be used again.

Faith stood beside Marcus, singing softly in the candlelight. All around her songs of hope and faith and love swirled in the air, and she started to understand just how intricately those three things were connected—just how they fed and supported each other—and she saw how poor she'd been in each until she'd met Marcus.

Heart pounding, she looked at his hand down by his side. It seemed to be waiting for something. Missing something. Slowly, keeping her breath in her throat, she slid her fingers into his. They fitted perfectly.

He started a little, but he caught her hand and held it firmly before she could react and pull away again. It felt so good it was all she could do to stop the tears sliding down her face. Finally that thing inside her that had always fluttered around like a trapped bird, making her restless, came to rest.

He didn't let go after the service. He kept her hand in his even though she knew she could have pulled away if she'd wanted to. People came up to congratulate him on resurrecting the old tradition, to tell him what a great time they'd had at the ball, and he smiled and chatted, all the time still holding her hand. She suspected he didn't want to let go in case she disappeared again.

Eventually the last person went out through the door and they were alone in the candlelit space.

She turned towards him and wound her other hand into his free one, tugged downwards to pull him towards her. He obliged, but stopped just short of kissing her, his lips hovering millimetres above hers. She closed her eyes and bridged the gap, softly exploring. In some ways it was like kissing him for the first time.

Even though she'd felt his skin beneath her fingers before, felt the touch of his lips on hers, part of her had been guilty of seeing him like a figure in her storybook—or in the windows she repaired. A noble knight or a prince. Beautiful, but not real. Not something she could have or hold. Or keep.

Marcus groaned and drew her close to him, kissed her both deeply and tenderly. This time she saw everything she'd missed before—the evidence of things she'd been too scared to hope for.

She pulled away and smiled at him. 'I'm sorry,' she said.

He just smiled back, making her knees feel like half-melted chocolate.

'You were right. I was running away. I was being a coward.'

He shook his head. 'I pushed too hard. I made you run.'

She wished she could let him take the blame, but she couldn't. 'No,' she said, looking into his eyes with frankness, making sure every last barrier had been smashed to the floor. 'You might have been right about the other stuff, but I said it was my choice, my mistake, and I was right about that.'

Marcus let out a soft little laugh. 'Okay. No arguing about that one.' He dipped his head and kissed her again. 'What matters is that you're back.'

'And I'm staying,' she added. 'If that's okay with you?'

Marcus growled, then kissed her soundly. She could have sworn she'd heard him mutter 'impossible woman' at some point.

'Oh…but I still need to go home for the holidays,' she said.

'I have things I need to say—to my sisters and to my mother… to my dad. Especially to my grandmother!'

He nodded. 'Of course you do,' he said. 'And I know it's not going to be an easy visit. That's why I'm coming with you—no arguments.' He reached for her hand. 'You don't have to do this on your own, Faith. Let *me* be the outsider for once.'

'I love you!' The words burst out of her before she could even think about stopping herself, but then she realised she didn't want to. 'Don't ever stop believing in me—even when I'm stupid enough to stop believing in myself.'

Marcus smiled that wolf-like smile of his before setting her down and stepping back. He gave her a look that sent a million volts charging through her, before dipping one hand in his pocket and pulling it out again. Faith couldn't see what he was holding. It was too dark in the candlelit chapel, and his fingers almost covered the small object.

It was only when he brought it up right in front of her face that she realised it was a box, and only when he eased it open and she saw a flash of candlelight reflected in its contents that she guessed its contents.

'That's…that's a…ring,' she stammered.

'I know,' Marcus said. 'Straight to the point, as always. That's my Faith.'

He took the ring from the box and held it out to her. It was stunning. An antique, she guessed. Art Deco, with a large square cut diamond.

'It's beautiful,' she said.

He blinked slowly. 'It was my grandmother's. I thought about giving you Evie's ring, but it has too much of a sad past. I wanted something connected with a lifetime of happy memories.'

She looked at the ring in its cushion. 'Marcus, I can't take this! It's a family heirloom! Some day somebody in your family might need to give it to the woman they want to marry.'

He stared at her, his eyebrows raised and an off-centre smile twisting one side of his mouth.

Oh.

Oh!

He just had.

The next day Faith woke in her turret room again. The light was so bright that she wondered if they'd another significant snowfall, but then she looked at the clock and realised it was halfway through the morning. She leapt out of bed and started getting dressed in so much of a flurry that she put her panties on the wrong way round. Twice.

Her flight was in less than two hours. They were never going to get to the airport in time!

Not bothering with socks and shoes, she bolted out of her room and ran down the large stone staircase, looking for someone. Anyone.

She found Bertie, sitting as usual in his armchair in the yellow drawing room.

'Plane!' she said breathlessly. 'Airport...'

'Do sit down, my dear,' he said, hardly looking up from his paper. 'Don't worry. Marcus has got it all under control.'

Faith did nothing of the sort. 'But—'

'And congratulations. I'm very much looking forward to having you as part of the family.'

That stopped her in her tracks. She looked down at the diamond on her left hand. In her panic she'd almost forgotten. She made herself take a deep breath before leaning over and kissing her soon-to-be grandfather-in-law on the cheek, smiling.

'Thank you,' she said, glancing out of the window. 'But about the plane...'

Bertie waved her away. 'Just go and finish getting dressed. Marcus will be back soon. And tell that boy I want a few great-grandchildren before I pop my clogs.'

She made herself take a deep breath before leaning over and kissing Bertie again.

'You're a meddling old man,' she said, smiling at him, 'and if I didn't know any better I'd think you and Gram had cooked this whole thing up together.'

That stopped her in her tracks. They *hadn't,* had they…?

But before she could interrogate him further Bertie flicked his newspaper, making it stand up straight.

'Didn't you say something about catching a plane?' he said, smiling like a cat. 'You might want to go and finish getting dressed.'

The plane! Gram was going to kill her if she didn't make it home for Christmas.

She ran back up to her turret bedroom and got herself packed as fast as she could. When she had just put her toothbrush back in her overnight bag the door opened.

'Ready?' Marcus said, but he didn't let her pick up her bag or leave the room. Instead he crossed the room and kissed her thoroughly.

Faith didn't resist at first, but then she started softly nudging his arm.

'What?' he said, as he bent to kiss one eyelid and then the other.

'We haven't got time for this!' she said. 'We've got to go. As it is I might miss the flight, and any chances of getting a standby at Christmas are practically non-existent!'

Marcus said as he reluctantly set her free, 'You mean *we* might miss the flight. I booked a ticket last night. I meant what I said about coming with you. Besides, I need to talk to your father about something while I'm there.'

And then he led an open-mouthed Faith out through the castle and onto the large oval lawn. Faith gasped when she saw what was sitting there.

'A helicopter?' she said, hardly able to take her eyes off the sleek machine.

'Quickest way to get to the airport,' he said, smiling.

When she got closer, she could see their luggage inside, and sitting on top of it all was Basil the badger, still with his red bow tied snugly around his neck. He looked ready for an adventure. Could stuffed badgers actually smile?

Faith reached over to stroke his head as she climbed inside and clipped herself into her seat. Then the blades began to whirr and the machine lifted itself straight up into the air, sending tiny ripples in every direction on the moat. She reached for Marcus's hand as the helicopter climbed higher in the air, banking slightly as it circled over the top of the lake and both islands, preparing to head off in the direction of the airport.

Faith looked down through the large window and her heart stalled. The castle looked even more beautiful from up here, with the turrets and chimneys reaching for them, the bright grass peeping from beneath the patchy snow. She felt a twinge of sadness at leaving it behind, even for a week or two.

Marcus leaned over and kissed her cheek, whispered in her ear. 'It won't be long before we're back,' he said.

She smiled at him, glad he was able to read her mind still.

'Good,' she said. 'Because I'm going to be looking forward to coming home. With you.'

She stopped smiling while she concentrated on the stinging at the backs of her eyes. She was *not* going to miss this wonderful view by spoiling it with tears. And she didn't mean the castle and lake below—she meant the wonderful man sitting next to her.

She leaned in and kissed him, not caring what the pilot thought.

He was hers, wasn't he? She just hadn't understood that, hadn't ever thought of it that way round. It wasn't just about her belonging to someone for it all to work, it had to be reciprocal.

'You're mine, Marcus Huntington,' she shouted at him over the noise of the blades. 'You belong to me now.'

He shook his head, took her hand, kissed it and looked deep into her eyes. 'No,' he mouthed, smiling. 'We belong to each other.'

* * * * *

COMING NEXT MONTH from Harlequin® Romance
AVAILABLE OCTOBER 30, 2012

#4345 THE COUNT'S CHRISTMAS BABY
Rebecca Winters
Forced apart by a devastating avalanche, Ric and Sami believed they'd lost each other forever...but this Christmas miracles do come true.

#4346 HIS LARKVILLE CINDERELLA
The Larkville Legacy
Melissa McClone
Will Hollywood actor Adam Noble finally take the biggest risk...throw away the script and open his heart to wardrobe assistant Megan Calhoun?

#4347 SLEIGH RIDE WITH THE RANCHER
Holiday Miracles
Donna Alward
Hope's looking for the perfect picture, but rancher Blake lives in a world of flaws. Is happiness somewhere in between?

#4348 MONSOON WEDDING FEVER
Shoma Narayanan
As the monsoons start, ex-college sweethearts Riya and Dhruv are forced to consider whether this wedding fever could perhaps be *contagious?*

#4349 THE CATTLEMAN'S SPECIAL DELIVERY
Barbara Hannay
Cattleman Reece had never held a baby until the night he saved pregnant Jess Cassidy and delivered her tiny daughter....

#4350 SNOWED IN AT THE RANCH
Cara Colter
When a wrong turn leads Amy and her baby son to Ty's ranch, they're snowbound together. But can they thaw Ty's heart?

You can find more information on upcoming Harlequin® titles, free excerpts and more at www.Harlequin.com.

HRCNM1012

REQUEST YOUR FREE BOOKS!
2 FREE NOVELS PLUS *2 FREE GIFTS!*

Harlequin Romance

From the Heart, For the Heart

YES! Please send me 2 FREE Harlequin® Romance novels and my 2 FREE gifts (gifts are worth about $10). After receiving them, if I don't wish to receive any more books, I can return the shipping statement marked "cancel". If I don't cancel, I will receive 6 brand-new novels every month and be billed just $4.09 per book in the U.S. or $4.49 per book in Canada. That's a savings of at least 14% off the cover price! It's quite a bargain! Shipping and handling is just 50¢ per book in the U.S. and 75¢ per book in Canada.* I understand that accepting the 2 free books and gifts places me under no obligation to buy anything. I can always return a shipment and cancel at any time. Even if I never buy another book, the two free books and gifts are mine to keep forever.

116/316 HDN FESE

Name	(PLEASE PRINT)	
Address		Apt. #
City	State/Prov.	Zip/Postal Code

Signature (if under 18, a parent or guardian must sign)

Mail to the **Reader Service:**
IN U.S.A.: P.O. Box 1867, Buffalo, NY 14240-1867
IN CANADA: P.O. Box 609, Fort Erie, Ontario L2A 5X3

Not valid for current subscribers to Harlequin Romance books.

**Are you a subscriber to Harlequin Romance books
and want to receive the larger-print edition?
Call 1-800-873-8635 or visit www.ReaderService.com.**

* Terms and prices subject to change without notice. Prices do not include applicable taxes. Sales tax applicable in N.Y. Canadian residents will be charged applicable taxes. Offer not valid in Quebec. This offer is limited to one order per household. All orders subject to credit approval. Credit or debit balances in a customer's account(s) may be offset by any other outstanding balance owed by or to the customer. Please allow 4 to 6 weeks for delivery. Offer available while quantities last.

Your Privacy—The Reader Service is committed to protecting your privacy. Our Privacy Policy is available online at www.ReaderService.com or upon request from the Reader Service.

We make a portion of our mailing list available to reputable third parties that offer products we believe may interest you. If you prefer that we not exchange your name with third parties, or if you wish to clarify or modify your communication preferences, please visit us at www.ReaderService.com/consumerschoice or write to us at Reader Service Preference Service, P.O. Box 9062, Buffalo, NY 14269. Include your complete name and address.

HRI1B

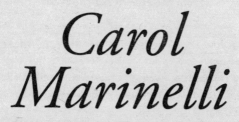

Discover the magic of the holiday season in
SLEIGH RIDE WITH THE RANCHER,
an enchanting new Harlequin® Romance story
from award-winning author Donna Alward.

Enjoy a sneak peek now!

* * *

"BUNDLE UP," he suggested, standing in the doorway. "Night's not over yet."

A strange sort of twirling started through her tummy as his gaze seemed to bore straight through to the heart of her. "It's not?"

"Not by a long shot. I have something to show you. I hope. Meet me outside in five minutes?"

She nodded. It was their last night. She couldn't imagine *not* going along with whatever he had planned.

When Hope stepped outside she first heard the bells. Once down the steps and past the snowbank she saw that Blake had hitched the horses to the sleigh again. It was dark but the sliver of moon cast an ethereal glow on the snow and the stars twinkled in the inky sky. A moonlight sleigh ride. She'd guessed there was something of the romantic in him, but this went beyond her imagining.

The practical side of her cautioned her to be careful. But the other side, the side that craved warmth and romance and intimacy…the side that she'd packaged carefully away years ago so as to protect it, urged her to get inside the sleigh and take advantage of every last bit of holiday romance she could. It was fleeting, after all. And too good to miss.

HREXP1112R

Blake sat on the bench of the driver's seat, reins in his left hand while he held out his right. "Come with me?"

She gripped his hand and stepped up and onto the seat. He'd placed a blanket on the wood this time, a cushion against the hard surface. A basket sat in between their feet and Blake smiled. "Ready?"

Ready for what? She knew he meant the ride but right now the word seemed to ask so much more. She nodded, half exhilarated, half terrified, as he drove them out of the barnyard and on a different route now—back to the pasture where they'd first taken the snowmobile. The bells called out in rhythm with hoofbeats, the sound keeping them company in the quiet night.

* * *

Pick up a copy of SLEIGH RIDE WITH THE RANCHER by Donna Alward in November 2012.

And enjoy other stories in the Harlequin® Romance **HOLIDAY MIRACLES** *trilogy:*

SNOWBOUND IN THE EARL'S CASTLE by Fiona Harper • Available now

MISTLETOE KISSES WITH THE BILLIONAIRE by Shirley Jump • December 2012

HARLEQUIN®

Discover the magic of Christmas with two
holiday stories of love and forgiveness in

CHRISTMAS IN TEXAS

Christmas Baby Blessings

by TINA LEONARD

Capri Snow isn't happy when she discovers
that the Bridesmaids Creek Christmastown Santa is her
almost-ex-husband and cop, Seagal West. But when danger
strikes, Seagal steps in to protect his wife, no matter the cost.

&

The Christmas Rescue

by REBECCA WINTERS

When Texas Ranger Flynn Patterson saves Andrea Sinclair
and her infant child from her stalker ex-husband, he finds
himself in more danger than just losing his heart.

Bring the magic of Christmas home
this November 2012.

Available wherever books are sold.

www.Harlequin.com

HAR75431

celebrating **15 YEARS**

Love Inspired

Kathryn Springer

inspires with her tale of a soldier's promise
and his chance for love in

The Soldier's Newfound Family

When he returns to Texas from overseas, U.S. Marine
Carter Wallace makes good on a promise: to tell a fallen
soldier's wife that her husband loved her. But widowed
Savannah Blackmore, pregnant and alone, shares a different
story with Carter—one that tests everything he believes.
Now the marine who never needed anyone suddenly
needs Savannah. Will opening his heart be the
bravest thing he'll ever do?

TEXAS TWINS

Available November 2012

www.LoveInspiredBooks.com

LI87776

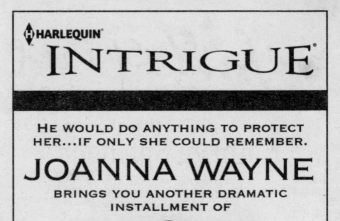